The War, Love, & Harmony Series:
Books 1 and 2

Fighting with the Infuriating Prince

and

Dancing with the Dangerous Prince

Elizabeth Lennox

Note: These books are free as e-books. Unfortunately, they cannot be free as paperbacks; printing has implicit costs. Learn more about the series or download the free books at ElizabethLennox.com.

CONTENTS

About the War, Love, and Harmony Series

This series encompasses two generations of love stories across the four fictional neighboring countries of Larcatia, Altair, Lurasa, and Tularia. When the four betrothed princes and princesses fall in love with the wrong partner, a devastating chain of events is set into motion. Only the future leaders can put things right.

The first two stories tell the tales of two princes and their unplanned romances.

Fighting with the Infuriating Prince: Jalayla couldn't believe the arrogance of the man! To actually order her around? How rude! But beneath the surface of her anger towards the handsome prince, there was a simmering heat, an uninvited fascination with the man that she couldn't seem to fight. Every time he touched her, every time he even looked at her, she felt that strange sensation.

Tasir wanted to fire her at first sight. She argued with him about everything and challenged him in ways that no other woman dared. So why did he want to pick the woman up and make love to her? Initially, he didn't know that the lovely woman with fiery eyes and a sensuous figure was the one and only Princess Jalayla. And was determined that he would have her for his own.

So what's a man to do when he finds out that the woman of his dreams is promised to marry another man?

Dancing with the Dangerous Prince: Jalayla couldn't believe the arrogance of the man! To actually order her around? How rude! But beneath the surface of her anger towards the handsome prince, there was a simmering heat, an uninvited fascination with the man that she couldn't seem to fight. Every time he touched her, every time he even looked at her, she felt that strange sensation.

1

Tasir wanted to fire her at first sight. She argued with him about everything and challenged him in ways that no other woman dared. So why did he want to pick the woman up and make love to her? Initially, he didn't know that the lovely woman with fiery eyes and a sensuous figure was the one and only Princess Jalayla. And was determined that he would have her for his own.

So what's a man to do when he finds out that the woman of his dreams is promised to marry another man?

Two weddings! Two love matches that weren't supposed to be! Princess Ciara of Altair, previously engaged to Prince Tasir went on to marry Prince Zoran of Larcatia. While Prince Tasir of Lurasa weds Princess Jalayla of Tularia.

Unfortunately, the weddings don't result in peace. The two couples were able to experience only a short-lived interlude of calm before tensions escalated to the point that violence was inevitable. Even after the weddings and despite years of trying to calm the problems, the four countries break out into war. A ten year, brutal war that was never supposed to be.

Sheik Zahir del Hassar Alzar of Larcatia brings the three other ruling sheiks to the Fortress of the Guards in secret. These four men – some recently risen to their power, others who have been rulers for a few years – all agree that it is time to stop the war caused by the tensions that were started when their parents or ancestors married years ago. The fighting has been going on too long and nothing has been gained. Borders remain as they were before the wars took place and the reasons for fighting don't seem to apply any longer. The broken marriage contracts never should have resulted in war; peace must be restored for the benefit of all four countries.

After long and challenging negotiations, the four rulers agree to cease hostilities and sign treaties so that the healing process can begin. They devise a strategy to help their people diffuse the rivalries and tensions that have developed. The four men agree that the best way to show their subjects that life should move on, without war, is to each marry and produce an heir. Royal weddings and the birth of a new generation will give the people a reason to hope.

The saga continues with another generation, where the now-current rulers of Larcatia, Altair, Lurasa, and Tularia must fulfill their treaty obligations.

The Sheik's Secret Bride: Their story began five years ago. Callie fell madly, crazily in love with Zahir. But the war in his country was raging and nurturing their relationship was tenuous at best. When Callie was captured, the experience was terrifying. Zahir found and rescued her, but he knew it would be impossible to insulate her from danger in his country. Despite his wishes to be together, he knew that to keep her safe he must send her away. However, he wouldn't let her go until she was his bride. In a secret wedding, he married her, and then spirited her to safety.

She arrived in her haven traumatized, fearful, homeless…and pregnant. Slowly, she rebuilt her life, gave birth to her son and somehow learned to get on with living without Zahir. For five long years, Callie recovered from the nightmare of her captivity. And she raises her son.

When Zahir enters her life once more, she can't believe that the fire between them is hotter than before. But she refuses to give in, despite its intensity. She's too afraid that the peace between the previously warring countries will end and that she or her son could be in peril again. She yearns to feel safe, but can she defy her heart or deny her son his father?

The Sheik's Angry Bride: Duty. Responsibility. Those were the priorities of Layla's upbringing. So when her father announced that she is to marry the Sheik of Lurasa, she accepted her duty and steeled her heart to a loveless life of obligation.

What she refused to accept was Garon's intense effect on her. The man wasn't what she anticipated! And he wouldn't conform to her plans or expectations. This was an arranged marriage! They had appearances to maintain, duties to adhere to. Why were these crazy feelings flying between them every time he touched her?

Garon entered into the marriage expecting only to be faithful to his wife and to the agreement he had made with the other sheiks. What he wasn't expecting was a fiery beauty that set his senses on fire or the intense need to have her. Responsibility be damned, this woman was his! And he was going to teach her about living and loving.

The Sheik's Blackmailed Bride: Luna couldn't believe the chain of events that had led to her wedding day. All she'd wanted was to save her small village, to help the residents to get out from underneath their crippling debt. So she'd written to the man who owned the bank. And here she was, walking down the aisle toward a man she barely knew. A man who could make her body sing but who could crush her hopes and dreams with a few harsh words.

Dassar needed a wife. The lovely Luna fit none of his criteria. She was too soft, too sweet and would be hurt by palace life. So why couldn't he forget her? Why could she get under his skin so easily? And why couldn't he simply walk away?

The Sheik's Convenient Bride: The only reason Kylie had come back to the palace was to prove to everyone that she was over Tarek. Her girlish infatuation was a thing of the past. So how did she end up dining with the sheik? And why was her body still vibrating when he kissed her? Why couldn't she simply put her infatuation in the past where it belonged?

Tarek took one look at the fascinating beauty and knew that Kylie was the woman he was going to have for his wife. He didn't want to marry, but the terms of the peace treaty were absolute. So if he had to do it, why not do it with the lovely, feisty and sexy woman that he couldn't get out of his mind?

Fighting with the Infuriating Prince: Chapter 1

"Get me a bottle of bourbon," the tall, dark man snapped to the woman fiddling with flowers as he burst into the previously soothing salon. The man leaned his hands against the back of the sofa, his arms spread wide and his head bowed low.

Jalayla spun around, shocked by the command and her eyebrows snapped up. How dare he speak to her like that! She looked behind her, realizing that he'd thought she was a servant because she'd been adjusting the floral arrangement, but it didn't matter. He shouldn't speak to servants like that either!

"Say please," she snapped right back, squaring her shoulders and lifting her chin defiantly.

With her sharp words, that muscular back tensed and his head came partway up. Not fully though. It was as if he might be tossing her response around in his head, thinking about her words, repeating them in his mind as if he couldn't believe she'd actually said them. To him.

Unconcerned, Jalayla crossed her arms over her stomach and glared, ignoring the creeping sensation of anxiousness that was coming over her.

But as the man stood up, his true height and brawn were revealed and she had to suppress her uneasiness. This was no regular man to be put in his place for an arrogant attitude. No, this man was of a completely different breed, she thought as she took in his broad shoulders and muscle packed arms that strained the tailored material of his shirt. She still couldn't see his face because he was turned away from her, but this man's body was enormous!

She shrank back slightly, but then realized what she was doing and stopped that action, refusing to let this man see her fear.

Then he swung around!

Goodness, he was gorgeous! All that black hair, cropped short but she could see how thick it was. His jaw already had a shadow of darkness to it even though he'd probably shaved only hours ago. And oh, he was tall!

And looking taller since he was walking towards her!

Jalayla refused to back down or back away. She absolutely would not allow this horrible, rude man to intimidate her! He'd been wrong to snap an order like that! She was right to point that out.

Those dark, almost black eyes traveled up and down her figure, stopping on her defiant features. "You're trembling. Good," he snapped. "Because you will be gone from here within the hour." He continued to walk closer, his eyes never leaving hers and he had to admit, he was impressed with her bravado. "Your employment here is at an end."

Jalayla's chin went up another notch, her soft, brown eyes glaring right back at him. "You're an idiot, sir. First of all, you don't have the authority to throw me out of the Fortress of the Guards, sir. This fortress was built on the land of four countries, all four of which control and manage this place. You do not have final authority to kick anyone out of the fortress. Secondly, if I'm to be thrown out of this fortress, it would be worth it to know that I won't ever have to deal with arrogant, conceited, rude and impolite jerks again!"

With that, she stepped around the enormous, terrifying man and headed for the doors. She would not stay in a room with this oaf another moment.

Tasir watched the woman with gleaming dark hair walk away from him, stunned by the surge of lust that hit him. And for a servant? Impossible! He never dallied with the help!

But she didn't hold herself like a servant. The woman daring to walk away from him was proud and confident. Damn, even the way she walked was making his body harden with desire for her. Or maybe it was just his need to eradicate impertinence in all forms.

Before she could step out of his reach, he grabbed her arm and spun her back around to face him. "Who are you?" he demanded. "I want a name!"

She had the audacity to try to jerk her arm out of his grip, but now that he was touching her, there was no way he was letting her go.

"Princess Jalayla bin Faisal of Tularia, at your service," she replied mockingly. She even added in a little curtsy, just for effect. "And who might be the man who is assaulting me?" she demanded. She recognized him, of course. This man was in the news much too often for her not to know who he was. She hadn't recognized him when he'd walked in and snapped an order at her, but as soon as she'd seen his face, she'd known who he was.

"Crown Prince Tasir Al Sharhi of Lurasa," he came right back and his eyes skimmed up and down her figure with thoroughness. "So you're the little Jalayla," he commented, moving closer but not releasing her arm.

Her eyes flared heatedly with his words and his continued hold onto her person. "I'm not little!"

His eyes flashed right back, standing so close that his shoes were almost touching hers. "You're little, and you're in danger of angering me, little one."

Her spine stiffened with those words. "Oh, and what are you going to do? Hit me? Are you such a big, mean man that you can't handle a woman's harsh words or honest opinion?"

He moved even closer, a full head taller than her, but she wasn't backing down. "You would be wise to watch your tongue," he warned, his voice soft and threatening.

She poked a finger in the middle of his chest, ignoring his words, knowing that she was courting danger but unable to stop herself. "I know the kind of man you are." She jerked her arm but he still wouldn't release her. "You're a big bully. You think that your height and your muscles make you stronger. But you can't rely on that all the time, you big oaf. At some point, intelligence is going to be required. And since you're severely lacking in that arena, you're going to fail."

Tasir had never met a man or a woman with the courage to question his intelligence. Hell, he'd never had anyone question him at all. "Would you care to put it to the test?"

She glared up at him, ignoring the crick in her neck. "I wouldn't want you to strain yourself."

There was a noise outside of the salon and he dropped her arm only moments before their fathers stepped into the room. Jalayla gave him one more fulminating glare before she turned to smile sweetly at her father as if nothing was bothering her in any way. Kissing his cheek, she walked out of the room, ignoring the tall, irritating man she knew was still glaring at her.

She dressed carefully for dinner that night. Already, she was regretting her outburst with Prince Tasir. Jalayla had no idea what had gotten into her. Sure, the man had snapped an order at her. But that was no reason to toss out insults. A simple, civil word explaining her title would have sufficed. She might have even gone so far as to gently reprimand him for the way he was speaking to the servants, but to call him names? That was beneath her.

She pulled her hair back so that it was smoothly out of her face, clipped it behind her and chose a blue dress to help calm her nerves. And hopefully his as well.

Jalayla stepped into the dining room that night and took a deep breath, bracing herself to face that man once again. At least her father and his would be with them this time. That would definitely temper their attitudes towards one another.

She spotted him immediately then looked around for her father and his. Unfortunately, the older men had not entered the dining room yet. Briefly, she considered turning around and waiting until the others could join the two of them, but Prince Tasir stopped her with his knowing gaze before she could move. She was trapped! His eyes moved up and down her figure, his gaze daring her to step into the dining room.

Taking another deep breath, she stepped further into the room. "Good evening, Your Highness. I would like to apologize for my behavior earlier this afternoon. It was inexcusable and inappropriate."

Tasir was stunned. And impressed. He had been fully prepared to resume their conflict where they'd left off before. And in an odd way, was he actually disappointed? He'd been bracing for another battle and she was conceding the war?

He could do nothing less. Bowing slightly, he followed her lead. "I was horribly rude as well, Your Highness. Please, call me Tasir and let us be finished with hostilities. Our countries have been friends for decades. We shouldn't be the ones to draw the battle lines."

Jalayla smiled and her shoulders relaxed, grateful that he was conceding as well.

She nodded to the servants and he pulled out her chair then waited for her to be seated before he moved to the opposite side of the table, taking his own seat. Picking up her wine glass, she struggled to find a non-controversial subject to discuss. "How is your mother?" she started off, almost groaning with the lameness of her conversational gambit.

"My mother is doing well," he replied, leaning back so that the servant could deliver the first course. "I will mention your inquiry to her."

Silence.

"And your uncle?" she prompted. "I know that he's been recovering from heart surgery."

Tasir almost laughed but he didn't want her to stop. She looked too adorable trying to come up with a topic to discuss that wouldn't devolve into an argument. "He, too, is doing well. Thank you for asking."

More awkward silence.

She carefully sliced up the crostini topped with caramelized onions and camembert cheese while she searched her brain for yet another topic for discussion. He certainly wasn't helping at all, she thought with increasing annoyance. "I've read several reports about the decline in violence in many of your urban areas. Congratulations. That must be a huge boon to your economy."

He took a taste of his crostini but wasn't really interested in the food. He found himself fascinated by the woman trying valiantly to control her temper even though he was doing everything he could to spark it. She was a charming woman, he thought. "The inhabitants of the urban areas are starting to find ways to amuse themselves other than causing problems."

That was all he was going to say? She dropped her eyes so that he couldn't see her temper. Taking a deep breath, she carefully laid her knife and fork down on the plate. "I'm sure that starting to eliminate poverty must make you and your father feel very proud," she offered.

Tasir shook his head. "Our policies only ease some of the people who fall below the middle class income level. There will never be any way to eradicate poverty. It is part of life."

Jalayla's heart fired up with those words. She worked hard to help the poverty-stricken areas of the capital city of Tularia. She showed up to help in the soup kitchens, talked to the various people who frequented those establishments and tried to find a solution that would help their plight.

"Isn't that a rather cynical outlook? As the future ruler of your country, shouldn't it be your goal to try and create a level playing field for all citizens?" She tried very hard to tamp down her anger, but the patronizing look he shot across the table zapped her patience.

"Your heart might be in the right place, princess, but your goals are unrealistic. Poverty is part of the world and will never be eliminated. We can only try to curb the violent tendencies of those who would prefer to live off of their illegal efforts and harm those that are more vulnerable, such as people in the lower income levels. Anyone who thinks that poverty can be stamped out is living in a fantasy world."

Jalayla stiffened. He was using her title in a patronizing manner and she didn't like it. Furthermore, he had no idea that he was insulting her personally since so many of her efforts were spent on helping the poor. But she couldn't let his words go. This was a subject on which she was very passionate. "Perhaps if rulers changed the way they viewed the world and the problems their citizens face, there would be more hope."

His eyes showed his amusement at what he perceived as a naïve outlook on the world. "Hope is a word that silly idealists use when they can't fix a problem." The first course was taken away and the second brought in. "Are you one of those bleeding hearts that think in communist terms but refuse to label yourself as a communist?"

She gasped because, yes, communism had proven to be a failure. "And you call yourself a leader? I doubt that the people living in the slums of Lurasa would agree with your outlook, sir."

He shook his head. "The people of Lurasa are well cared for because they have leaders like me who know what is realistic and helpful and don't try to achieve ridiculous dreams that have been tried throughout history – tried and failed," he emphasized.

She almost stumbled over her words in an effort to defend her ideals. "I can't believe that someone in your position doesn't believe that poverty can be eliminated. And it never will be when you won't even believe in the possibility."

He picked up his spoon but didn't sample the soup, too intent on the argument. She was beautiful when she was riled up. "Name one time in history when there has been no poverty."

She squared her shoulders, fully engaged in the argument now. "Name one time in history when leaders have been selfless enough to honestly strive for it!" she countered.

"Exactly," he returned. "Leaders, not just political leaders but business and social leaders, don't want poverty to end. At a very basic level, people need to know that they are better than someone else. It is an innate need to feel superior to others. Call it an instinct for survival or whatever, but it is strong and isn't going away. Therefore, poverty will always be around."

He had a valid point, but she wasn't backing down on hers either. "An equal playing field should still be the goal."

Tasir shook his head. "At its deepest level, humanity doesn't want an equal playing field. You're just trying to redefine…"

"Don't you dare call me a communist again!" she almost shouted at him.

"Idealist," he finished after her outburst, suppressing his laughter at her disgruntled expression. "Come to the real world, princess. And maybe you'll make more of a difference."

She was practically shaking with her fury. "I suppose that you think women should be barefoot and pregnant and shouldn't be stealing jobs that your unequal playing field has yet to create? Isn't it nice that most of your policies educate and promote men and leave more than half of your population defenseless? Not the best way to eliminate poverty but a good start at helping half of your citizens with their innate need to feel better than someone else, right?"

His eyebrows drew down over his eyes with those words. "The women of my country have just as much opportunity to attend school as any man."

She shook her head, unaware of how soft wisps of her lovely, dark hair danced against her creamy complexion. "No! And what's worse is that you have no idea that you're promoting men over women with every law you pass. Do you purposely deny women any say in the political process or are you just stopping it by not letting them into the schools so they don't even know how to read an election ballot?"

He wasn't letting her get away with that accusation. "The literacy rates in my country are higher than in many other countries," he came right back.

She moved forward in her chair, really getting into the argument now. "What are the discrepancies between the rates of males and females? Is there an equal distribution of girls and boys in the classroom? And in the classroom, are the girls allowed to sit in the front of the class or are they relegated to the back?"

"Gender bias is decreasing but it is a slow process. We cannot combat centuries of discrimination in one generation. You're determined to only see the wrong in the world."

Her eyes widened with that accusation. "I thought you just called me an idealist?" she argued right back.

"I think you're a very passionate woman with a skewed view of the world," he countered.

Jalayla realized suddenly that she was virtually shouting!

She took a deep breath and hid her hands underneath the table. "This conversation has gotten out of control," she said in a much more even tone.

Tasir was astonished for two reasons. First of all, she had a point and he was furious that her ideas hadn't been brought to his attention before this moment. And secondly, his body was hard as a rock, ready to lift her up and make love to her right here on the dining room table.

He couldn't believe that he was turned on by this woman once again. He'd thought that this afternoon had been a fluke. He didn't like argumentative, opinionated women. He preferred ladies who were soft and ready to please and accept pleasure. This woman sitting across from him would more than likely stab him than make love with him.

"I think I've had enough for the night," she said and stood up. "I apologize for abandoning the meal, but perhaps it would be better if we just went our separate ways." And with that, she walked out of the dining room with her head held high and her shoulders stiff.

Tasir cursed under his breath as his erection started throbbing with the view of her very round, very delectable looking derriere as she departed. He pulled his eyes away, thinking he'd like to paddle that bottom. But that only caused him to groan out loud at the image of her body lying across his, that bottom right there for his eyes to feast upon. Oh yes, he'd spank her. And then he'd make love to her until she didn't have the energy to argue with him any longer.

With that image in his mind, he stood up and walked into the salon attached to the dining room. Pouring himself a large portion of scotch, he downed it in one swallow. He hissed as the burn slid down his throat and he could even feel it in his chest. Damn that woman!

Chapter 2

Jalayla lay in her bed, staring up at the ceiling. That man just made her so angry! He was pompous and arrogant and wouldn't accept that she might have a point! No concessions in any way!

And to call her an idealist! Oh, that was low! She might have lofty goals, but she truly believed that she could make a difference. If everyone helped out, the world could definitely be a better place.

And she was hungry! She'd skipped lunch because of their afternoon encounter and she'd barely eaten anything over dinner because of their evening argument.

Snapping the sheets back, she glanced at the clock. It was after two o'clock in the morning and she was starving. She would never be able to get to sleep with this aching emptiness. Or the anger.

A cup of hot milk would help.

She grabbed her silk robe and walked over to the wall. Her fingers traced the moldings, looking for the switch. She hadn't been through this secret passage in years but she knew the lock was around here somewhere. A moment later, her fingers slid over the secret latch! With a snick, the wall opened up. Slipping into the hallway, she peered around but it was too dark to venture further. She ran back to her bedroom and found a flashlight and slippers. No way was she going in there without a flashlight. Talk about creepy things! A dark, closed off tunnel was the thing nightmares were made of.

Slipping through the secret passageway, she refused to think about how dark it was behind her. She and her best friend, Princess Ciara from Altair, had come to this fortress so many times and they'd traveled through these tunnels, making sure they knew all of them. They'd never told anyone else, although she was fairly sure that someone else must know about them.

It took her a couple of wrong turns, but eventually she found the secret door that led to the fortress kitchen. Pushing it open, she slipped into the darkened room, looking around to make sure no one else was present.

Sure enough, the night crew was finished and the morning team hadn't started yet. They would probably be here in a few hours, ready to start preparations for the morning meal. But right now, she was free to grab the ice cream that was in the freezer. She grabbed some cheese and crackers as well, and a bottle of wine. No need to go for the warm milk when a glass of excellent wine might have the same effect.

Sitting down with the ice cream on her right, the cheese and crackers to her left and the glass of wine front and center, she perched on a stool and enjoyed her middle of the night feast.

The ice cream soothed all of her frustrations and the wine went perfectly with the sharp cheese. She knew that this was the best meal she'd had in a long time.

Until the deep, gravelly voice interrupted her.

"Not the healthiest meal I've ever seen," the deep voice said from the kitchen doorway. "But I'm guessing it is delicious."

Jalayla twisted on the stool she'd pulled up to the counter, her breath catching in her throat when she spotted Prince Tasir, without a shirt and wearing only a pair of jeans that rode very low on his hips. And bare feet. Goodness, those bare feet looked…

Jalayla was having trouble breathing as he pushed away from the doorway where he'd obviously been watching her. Walking towards her, he looked like some sort of body builder with all of those bulging muscles on his arms and shoulders, those ridges in his stomach. She wasn't aware of her mouth falling open as she watched him approach.

Tasir couldn't believe his eyes. When he'd walked into the kitchen, there she was. No longer was she dressed in the formal blue gown from the evening or the stiff suit he'd first seen her in this afternoon.

Instead, she was draped in rose silk that smoothed over her figure, making his erection fire up once again. Not that it had ever really gone away. He no longer needed to figure out what it was about her that drove him so nuts. It wasn't her fiery tongue or the flashing brown eyes. Nope. It was her figure. Those full, soft breasts were pressing against the silk, her nipples forming beads under the material that made his mouth ache to taste and feel with his tongue. Her waist was slight but then her hips flared out into a perfect hourglass, making him want to slide his hands down so he could cup the round softness of her bottom.

He took a deep breath and tried to regain control of his raging libido. Never had he been this affected by a woman. "Hungry?" he asked her, trying to figure out what it was about her that caused such an impact.

Tasir didn't wait for a response. He simply grabbed her delicate wrist, pulling the spoonful of now-melting ice cream to his mouth and devoured the sweet treat, just as he wanted to do to her. As he looked down into her startled, brown eyes, he was certain that she would taste much better than the ice cream.

"Put a shirt on!" she snapped, whipping out of her perusal of all those magnificent muscles.

"No," he countered and took her wine glass. Lifting it to his mouth, he downed the entire contents. When he was done, he put the glass back on the counter behind her.

"Move back!" she gasped, leaning against the metal counter because he was so close.

He leaned in even closer. "Make me," he challenged.

Jalayla fisted her hands, trying to resist the temptation to press her fingers against that bare chest. She was absolutely not interested in feeling those muscles, she promised herself. And she wasn't enthralled by that dark hair or the flat, male nipples that…

"You're crowding me," she told him angrily.

She stood up but he trapped her even more effectively by putting a hand on either side of her, flat on the metal counter behind her. "So push me away," he told her, his voice husky and sexy and oh-so-amazing.

"I'm not touching you," she snapped back at him but she was having trouble tearing her eyes away from that chest.

"I get it," he told her with a smug expression to his handsome face.

She didn't like the sound of that. "What do you think you understand? You don't understand me at all. You're too arrogant to understand anyone but yourself!"

He leaned in even more and she gasped when she felt his strong hands at her waist. She grabbed his wrists, trying to push him away. But he ignored her efforts and simply lifted her up onto the counter. "What the hell did I do to make you so angry?" he demanded. He grabbed another glass from the shelf behind him and poured wine into both. "I'm a nice guy."

Jalayla shivered as she curled her legs up onto the countertop. He stole her stool and, from the hard look in his eyes, she suspected that he wasn't going to let her down off of the counter until she talked to him.

"It's late."

"And it's going to get a whole lot later. You'd better start trying to figure out how we're going to get along with each other because I have a whole week here with your father and mine. So unless you're going to turn tail and run, we're going to be running into each other over the next several days."

She stared up at him for a pregnant moment before reaction set in. "You can't be here for the whole week!" she gasped. "You have to be at that stupid conference in Dubai!"

He shook his head and sipped the wine. "Nope. My father sent his aide. He wanted me here."

She clamped her lips shut.

He chuckled at her adorable expression. "Drink your wine and tell me why you're such an uptight snob."

Her shoulders stiffened even more at those words. "I am not a snob!" she gasped. "And I am certainly not uptight! Just because I don't appreciate the lumbering efforts of an enormous oaf to manhandle me, that gives you no right to pass judgment on me."

"You've already passed judgment on me. Fair play to throw it right back at you." He tossed a cracker into his mouth.

She glared back at him indignantly, then grabbed the spoon and delved into the softened ice cream. "Is it so bad that someone on this planet doesn't think you're the most amazing man in the world?"

"That would be fine, if you were the kind of female that respected men."

She rolled her eyes. "I respect men when they're considerate and kind." Jalayla pulled her eyes away from the blue-black hair that seemed to be reflecting the overhead lights of the kitchen. He wasn't good looking, she reminded herself. He was just a man, and not a nice one at that. If her eyes wandered to his broad, muscular shoulders, it was the same reaction she'd have if staring at an interesting statue. No, she clarified, the statue she could appreciate. This man just exasperated her.

He chuckled, shaking his dark head. "No. You only deal with men when you can walk all over them. I bet you're one of those women who would prefer men to be subservient to women."

She huffed as she swallowed another bite of ice cream. "I don't hate men. I think there should be equal respect on both sides. That's a foreign concept to you though. Too hard dealing with a woman who can think and walk at the same time?" she taunted, blinking her long lashes rapidly.

They sparred back and forth until the cheese and crackers were gone, the bottle of wine emptied and the ice cream half gone. Jalayla would like to say that he'd eaten most of the food and yes, he'd made a significant dent in that feast, but she'd certainly helped. She wasn't even hungry but there was a strange, clawing need inside of her that couldn't be assuaged. The longer they argued, the more she ate.

She put the lid firmly on top of the ice cream, trying to get herself to stop eating. "Just because men are stronger, that doesn't mean that they're better."

He stood up abruptly and leaned over her. "Do you really believe that a stronger person doesn't have an advantage in this world?" he asked. At the same time, his hand slipped onto her ankle, exposed by her now-relaxed pose.

Jalayla's breath caught and her eyes widened. She opened her mouth to say something, but his fingers moved again and whatever she'd been about to say simply fluttered out of her mind. Shaking her head, she tried to move her leg out of his grasp but his fingers closed over the delicate bones.

She re-focused on their argument, unwilling to let him think he'd won. "Strength definitely has an advantage in the short term, but long term, it is going to take…"

She didn't have a chance to finish that sentence. His eyes moved away from her face, down to her legs. Her mind stopped thinking completely as his long fingers stroked her calf, moved down to her toes and her feet. Those strong fingers pressed into the strained muscles of her feet and she closed her eyes as erotic sensations shot through her whole body.

She wasn't aware of how her head fell backwards. But Tasir was. The entire time they'd been arguing with each other, he had been painfully aware of her nipples pressing against the silk of her robe. When he pressed his fingers into the arch of her foot, something shot right through her body. Jalayla's breath left her body in a whoosh, her hands fisting against the countertop. She opened her mouth to beg him to stop, but then his strong fingers moved again against her foot.

She was completely unaware of the way her back arched whenever he pressed his fingers against her foot. But Tasir was completely aware of all of the signs that she was unconsciously broadcasting. His eyes missed nothing as her body trembled against his hands, his fingers absorbing each of her shivers as he worked the muscles in her feet. Not many people knew all of the erogenous zones that were centered in the foot, but he'd learned through experience, trial and error. His triumph was in watching the expressions on her face as her body came alive from his touch.

"What are you doing to me?" she whispered with more than a touch of desperation.

Tasir stood up, his hands sliding up her legs and bringing the silk of her nightgown right along with them. "You have been tormenting me ever since the moment we met this afternoon. I'm just giving back a little bit of what you've done to me."

"I haven't done anything to you," she said as she shivered. His hands slid higher, pausing against her knee. When his fingers tickled the back of her legs her eyes opened up and she stared into his eyes. "So is this proving that you're stronger?"

His eyes moved down to her legs, noticing how soft and smooth her skin was. "Oh no, this is retribution. Pure and simple retribution."

Her hands had been holding her up as she leaned back against the countertop. But when his hands started to move further up her legs, she gave up that position and grabbed his wrists, so startled by the feelings zinging through her with his hands moving onto skin that no man had ever touched before. She couldn't handle this. Her head shook back and forth, denying him any further movement.

"We can't do this," she told him, her eyes wide with both amazement and need, but also laced with fear and confusion.

His dark eyes moved from her beautiful features down to her breasts, noting the twin peaks that were pressing against the silk of her nightgown and robe. "Oh, we're going to do this and so much more."

She shook her head. "No, we can't."

"Give me one good reason," he demanded softly.

It was a struggle to try and think or even form words with her mouth. Jalayla was desperate to stop his hands. She didn't understand what was happening to her. Didn't she hate this man? Wasn't he the enemy?

If he was the enemy, how could he so easily make her feel like this?

She opened her mouth to try and tell him why this was such a bad idea but instead of the words coming out, his mouth covered hers. She felt his tongue invade her mouth, and then a moan escaped from deep inside of her. When her arms released his wrists and wrapped around his neck, Jalayla had no idea that she'd actually moved her arms. All she knew was that his hands were now gripping her hips, pulling her closer. He wouldn't stand for her attempts at keeping her legs closed. At the same time that she felt his large, strong hands on her hips, his own hips had already moved between her legs. There was an unfamiliar hardness pressing against her heat that she'd never felt before. There was also an inexplicable sense of urgency, an ache that she couldn't seem to ease no matter how much she shifted against that hardness. In fact the more she shifted, the more intense the ache became.

She heard some strange sounds, but had no idea that she was actually the one making the noises. All she knew was that she needed to assuage this driving need that was centered right down in her core, right where that hardness was pressing against her.

One moment, she had been arguing with this man and the next moment she was in his arms, her fingers fisting in his hair while his hands moved slowly over her body. That ever-increasing ache was driving her crazy. Every cell in her body was shifting, trembling, shivering in an effort to find a way to stop this ache. So when that strong hand moved from her bottom up underneath her nightgown to discover her breast, she was shocked by what she was feeling. Fortunately, she didn't have enough time to become concerned or stop his hand. His experienced fingers quickly found her nipple. When that thumb and forefinger started exploring the sensitive nub, her entire body exploded into a swirl of pleasure unlike anything she'd ever experienced in her entire life.

The waves of pleasure surrounded her, pulsed around her body, centered at that secret part of her that no man had ever touched before. She couldn't believe how amazing the sensations felt and didn't want to open her eyes for fear that the feelings would stop. But eventually, they slowed down and finally the muscles in her body felt like molten lava, her limbs unable to hold herself upright any longer and she faded to the countertop.

When she opened her eyes, she found Tasir staring down at her with a look in his eyes that made her whole body start to tremble again.

"What just happened?" She asked with a voice that she didn't recognize.

Tasir's hand slid down her body enjoying the way that she shifted against him. Watching her come apart in his hands was almost worth the pain that he was feeling with the unsatisfied ache of his erection.

"I believe that you have just experienced your first orgasm."

Jalayla jerked against him, pulling away from his body. She would have fallen off of the counter if he hadn't caught her and placed her on her feet. Tasir's hands held her until she regained her balance. But when she could see straight once again, she stepped backwards out of his arms.

With as much dignity as she could muster, she smoothed her hands down the sides of her robe, ensuring that she was adequately covered. "No, that couldn't have happened," she said and quickly retied the silk of her robe back around her. "I have to go."

She literally ran out of the kitchen and down the hallways back to her room. Slamming the door closed behind her, she leaned against the heavy wood and closed her eyes. Embarrassment and humiliation swept over her as she thought back to what she had just done in his arms.

Her shaking hands covered her face as the tears started to flow. Never in her life had she ever done anything as crazy and promiscuous as what she'd just experienced in the arms of a man that she thought she disliked so intensely.

Jalayla crawled into bed and pulled the covers up over her head. Hugging the pillow against her, she let the tears of humiliation flow, knowing that no one else would see her shame.

Chapter 3

Jalayla loosened the reins, allowing the horse underneath her to gallop across the desert. She'd woken up late this morning, missing breakfast with her father. She knew that she had done something so horribly wrong – something that she could never take back.

Her only objective this morning was to get away, to ride out into the desert so that she could try and put last night's activities into perspective.

She would have to go home. There was absolutely no way that she could ever face Tasir again. Not after what he had done to her last night. He knew secrets about her, about her body, that she never wanted anyone else to know about. He had so easily changed her from a cool, intelligent, respectable lady into a wanton woman with no scruples, no inhibitions, no moral code.

That was not who she was. That was not even who she wanted to be.

She felt the horse's energy start to dissipate and slowed him down. Looking out into the desert, she knew that she had done something wrong. That didn't mean that her whole life had been ruined though. Last night, things hadn't gone far enough for that to have happened. She definitely didn't wanted to run into him again, but she sighed as she accepted that no real damage had been done. Except to her pride.

The man was diabolical. He had done things to her that she'd never thought were possible.

She turned the horse around and started walking back towards the fortress. Not that she was going to go back there. Oh no, there was no way that she could face her father right now – not to mention the man who had created those feelings inside of her.

She walked her horse around the fortress, ignoring the guards who stood sentry at the gates. She waved to them and indicated that she was going around the perimeter and they nodded their understanding.

At a trot, she rode from the desert around to the rear of the fortress where the terrain changed from sand to shrubs and then into short trees and finally, to taller trees. As she climbed higher up into the mountains, the terrain turned into a lush, evergreen environment. The mountains created such a high terrain that the trees were able to get a small amount of moisture from the clouds, so it was only evergreens that grew. Deciduous trees couldn't grow in this kind of harsh environment because they couldn't retain enough water. But the strong, drought resistant evergreens created a forest of color that was different from almost anywhere else in this area.

She followed the pathway that would lead her to her favorite place. And when she found it, she released the reins of the horse and let him wander over to a small crop of grass where he could nibble.

The cool stream formed a pool here that was surrounded by the trees, creating a little oasis, although with evergreens instead of palm trees. She'd come here whenever she could as a kid, swimming and laughing in the water, playing hide and seek in the trees or just lying on the ground, staring up at the clouds. Those had been halcyon days, when her biggest worry was learning to sit still during diplomatic dinners.

Taking off her boots, she let her feet dangle into the cool water. Almost no one knew about this area. She and Princess Ciara had discovered it a long time ago.

She reached down and let her fingers trail in the cool water. But it still wasn't enough. As her face flamed with color and she remembered what she'd done last night with Tasir, she wondered if she could just strip off all of her clothes and swim in the cool water. It seemed like such a great idea, to just purify herself in the water. She knew that it was a silly thought because nothing could cleanse her soul or get rid of the memories of how Tasir had made her feel. But the idea of swimming in the water, of releasing all of the strict rules that had been put upon her as she'd grown up, all of the etiquette that had been drilled into her over the years, gave her a sense of freedom.

She and Ciara had often smuggled bathing suits to this place, swimming in the cool water on the hot afternoons when they'd spent weeks here during the summers.

What would be the harm? No one else knew about this place.

Surely it was safe. Wasn't it?

Jalayla stood up and looked around. She felt a little silly because, really, who else would be here? The only people that were around the fortress were her father, the Sheik of Lurasa, and Tasir. Well, and all of the servants. But there would be no reason for them to be stepping out of the fortress at this point during the day. Besides, none of them would actually come up into the mountains like this. This was a hidden trail, and a hidden water area.

She was being ridiculous. If she wanted to go swimming, she should just take off her clothes and go swimming. There was really no reason why anyone would see her up here. And even if someone had a pair of high-powered binoculars, no one could see through the trees to this point.

Again, she felt silly and decided to just go for it. It was a scorching hot day and she wanted to swim. She wanted to be free of her guilt over what she had done last night and her shame at how glorious it had felt.

She resolutely stood up and started unbuttoning her shirt. Dropping it to the ground, she slithered out of her riding pants and folded them up on top of her shirt. Looking around one more time, just to be sure, she reached behind herself and unfastened the clasp of her bra. Down it fluttered to the growing pile of clothes and then her underwear as well.

She didn't stand on the rock too long, knowing that she was completely naked. Even though she had assured herself that no one was around, and no one could look at or see her, she still moved quickly into the water. As the cool liquid surrounded her overheated body, she felt the tension of the past twelve hours seep out of her. It felt so wonderful to just slide into the water, not having a care in the world. At least for the moment.

She swam back and forth, enjoying the water and splashing about. She remembered so many times sliding down into the water with Ciara, talking about what their futures were going to be like when they grew up. Never in her wildest imagination would she have thought that she would come to a point in her life where she was hiding from a man with whom she had done such intimate things and felt so ashamed.

She was floating on her back, slowly kicking her feet as she stared up into the sky, peering at the clouds through the tops of the trees. Jalayla was completely unaware of the man standing on the rock right next to her clothes, watching her and enjoying the spectacle.

"Are you doing this to torment me again?" Tasir demanded in a deceptively lazy tone of voice.

Jalayla twirled about, sputtering as she flung her body around, trying to find the owner of that deep voice, praying that it wasn't the one man she'd been avoiding all day even as she tried to hide her nakedness, all at the same time. Not an easy feat, she realized as she accidentally swallowed a large mouthful of water.

It couldn't be.

She simply wasn't that unlucky in life, was she?

She searched the edge of the water, her eyes widening as she took in the man standing right next to her clothes.

"Go away. You're not supposed to be here."

Tasir continued to watch her. Well, he continued to watch her breasts underneath the crystal waters of the stream. He had watched those breasts, wondered about the color and size of her nipples last night over and over as they'd argued about so many subjects. It was astonishing to realize that he'd enjoyed talking and arguing with this woman as much as he'd enjoyed watching her melt in his arms. Her eyes flashed when she was climaxing just as they did when she was heatedly arguing her point. And she had several valid arguments too. She wasn't just a pretty face. A rare combination that incited his lust.

His fingers had felt those nipples for only a brief moment before she had pulled away from him. Now, he was feasting on the view of those perfect, pink nipples underneath the water. And there was no way that he was going to look away.

"I didn't know that you had any ownership of the stream," he retorted.

She crossed her arms over her chest, forcing his eyes to move upwards and focus only on her eyes. "You're not welcome here," she almost yelled at him. "Go away."

Even from this distance she saw the sardonic eyebrow rise at her command and knew that he was going to ignore her words. That same sensation that she'd experienced last night started tingling low in her belly, moving downwards to that secret place between her legs that she was so mortified of.

"Under the circumstances, you can't really expect me to follow that order, can you?"

Jalayla gritted her teeth at his continued refusal to back away. "Fine! You can have the stream. Just turn around so I can dry off and get dressed."

He shook his head, telling her in no uncertain terms that he was not moving. "Give me one good reason why I should."

Under other circumstances, perhaps when his heated gaze wasn't searching through the water as he tried to see her nakedness, Jalayla knew that her brain would be able to function properly. But as he stood there, his feet planted firmly apart in an aggressive stance, she shivered with all of those embarrassing, terrifying feelings she knew she should ignore. So her brain wasn't functioning at full capacity and the combination of her nakedness, his look, and those annoyingly broad shoulders was bringing whatever brain efficiency she normally had to rock bottom levels. "Because you're a gentleman."

Once again, that irritating man simply shook his head.

Her mouth fell open in shock at his response. "Are you seriously telling me that you're not a gentleman?"

Those firm lips that had been set in a straight line, slowly quirked upwards into a smile that tightened the muscles in her stomach. "At what point during our short relationship have you ever mistakenly thought of me a gentleman?"

He had a valid point. Jalayla wanted to stomp her feet in frustration, but she was in the water and stomping wasn't as effective. Besides, it was childish and pointless. She had to focus all of her energy on getting out of this situation.

Unfortunately, she didn't have a chance to focus on anything except Tasir. Because, a moment later, her startled eyes caught him starting to unbutton his own shirt. "What are you doing?" she demanded nervously.

He shrugged out of his shirt and she couldn't stop her eyes as they drifted down to that amazing chest that she'd seen last night. A part of her wished that she had explored that magnificent expanse of muscle and skin but she had been too overwhelmed with all of the other sensations that had been ripping through her and she hadn't taken advantage of that opportunity.

When his fingers moved to his belt she gasped and actually took a step backwards. "What are you doing?" She had to use her arms to regain her balance because she'd stumbled over a hidden rock in the water. But as soon as she had reestablished herself, she pulled her arms back around her body and re-covered her breasts.

"Did you do that on purpose?" she demanded.

Tasir chuckled, the sound deep and sexy. "I wish that I had been able to anticipate that movement because I would have had a better look. But no worries," he said as his fingers moved to his riding boots. He pulled them off and set them next to her own riding boots. Jalayla couldn't stop the comparison of his extremely large boots right next to her smaller ones. And then her eyes moved back to his body and the comparison was even more pronounced.

"You don't want to do this," she told him in a quivering voice.

"Oh, yes I do. It's a hot day and the water looks very refreshing. Very inviting."

She gasped as he moved his fingers back to his belt buckle, unhooked it, and deftly slid the zipper down. "At least leave your pants on," she begged.

"You didn't," he replied. And in a whoosh his pants were discarded, boxers and all. "What are you doing?" she demanded with a gasp of horror. Or was it fascination?

"What does it look like I'm doing?" he asked. "Why would you even question something like this? The water is more inviting today than I've ever seen it in my entire life."

"You know about this place?" she asked

"Of course I know about this place. I've swum here many times – whenever I came to the fortress."

There went her assumption that she was the only one, besides Ciara, who knew about it. Apparently, it wasn't as secret as she'd thought it was.

For each step that he took closer to her, she took a step backwards. She was unaware that her mouth was hanging open in amazement and awareness. But Tasir was painfully aware of those soft, beautiful, brown eyes moving down his body. Her eyes were almost a caress as she looked at each part of his chest. When he noticed her eyes pausing at his erection, he stopped and waited, letting her look her fill.

He didn't want to scare her, but the more she looked, the more his body ached to take her into his arms and make her his woman. It was an insane thought to have, but he couldn't get it out of his mind. His eyes moved down her body and noticed that her hands and arms were relaxing. Before, her hands had been covering those beautiful breasts that he so wanted to see. But now they were falling lower. He still wasn't able to see the perfect, pink nipples but soon – very, very soon.

As she continued to watch, he moved into the water, his eyes never leaving her face. Slowly, he walked into the water and, when she could no longer see that fascinating part of him, her eyes rose up to his and she almost stumbled backwards again on the rock that was determined to foil her plans to stay out of this man's arms.

Tasir saw her start to fall backwards and he quickly eliminated the last two feet between them, pulling her into his arms so that she was against him, exactly where he wanted her.

Jalayla gasped as he lifted her higher, his strong arms and the buoyancy of the water helping to reveal her body to this man. She dangled in front of him, her body trembling as she waited to see what he would do.

"Take your arms away, Jalayla," he ordered.

She shook her head. "I can't," she whispered, not really able to explain why she couldn't, just knowing that revealing her breasts to his hungry gaze would stir that wild ache that seemed to be throbbing between her legs.

He didn't ask again. Instead, he lifted her higher, his concentration focusing on another, more fascinating goal. When she realized his intent, she gasped and covered that area instead, leaving her breasts free and right in front of his face. He took advantage of her change and nuzzled one perfect breast with his nose and his mouth. When he took her pink nipple into his mouth, Jalayla was no longer able to cover herself. Her hands whipped up to his head, holding him in place while her body arched into his mouth, causing him to take her nipple deeper. He sucked on that tender flesh and she screamed out, shocked by the intensity of feeling that shot right down to her core.

Unconsciously, she wrapped her legs around his waist, her body no longer trembling with fear but with a hunger, a passion that she didn't understand. Last night had been crazy but this, what he was making her feel…it was like an urgent, intense pulsing that made her out of control.

Tasir heard the sexy sounds and reacted to them as if they were a lightning bolt. He moved over to the other nipple, enjoying the way she was now rubbing against his body. She was trying to move lower, to instinctively find that elusive solution to her problem, but with her body up in the air like this, she wasn't going to find it.

"Tasir, I can't…"

"You can," he countered before she could speak the words. He was already walking over to the edge of the water. He held her in his arms, kissing her the whole time. He spread his shirt out on the ground, then laid her down, he looked at her and almost lost that famous control that so many had cursed.

He watched her body shift with unconscious invitation and couldn't hold back. He bent lower, his big body already between her legs and he nibbled his way down to that perfect place. When his tongue touched her, she sat up with a shocked sound but he didn't relent. His body was aching to have her but he also wanted this experience to be the best of her life. So when he continued his ministrations, she cried out as her back once again melted to the shirt. A split second later, her hips were lifting up, almost offering herself to him and he took full advantage of that movement, sliding his hands underneath her round bottom and lifting her higher, his mouth moving against that sensitive place, ignoring her hands that tried to push him away. He didn't let up until he felt her body convulse.

The sight and taste of her splintering apart like that drove away all remnants of control. Moving back up her body, he took her hands, lifting them so that they were once again around his neck. "You're mine, Jalayla," he growled a moment before he pressed into her soft flesh. When she stiffened slightly in his arms, he cursed himself. "I'm sorry," he groaned, regretting his too-powerful invasion. This gentle, sweet woman was a virgin. Or she had been. And he'd known that! He should have gone slower, taken more care. He should have…

"Please don't stop," she said with a breathless sound, her hips shifting against his. "Oh, please don't!" And her back arched against him, trying to take him deeper. "Is this…"

"No," he laughed, the sound showing the pain he was in caused by going so slowly with her. "That's not all." He was so turned on by this woman, never had he felt this way. Women were always very nice to hold and he had a strong sexual appetite, but never had a woman caused him to lose control like this.

But he wasn't fighting it. He shifted slightly, testing to make sure she really was okay. When her mouth fell open and her eyes softened, he knew that she was fine. Better than fine!

He moved again, sliding in and out of her heat. Over and over again, he shifted into her tight sheath, watching her eyes. When he felt the bite of her nails in his shoulders, his control almost slipped again. He could feel her tightening around him, felt her body shiver only moments before she screamed out, her climax washing over her once again. And with that, he could no longer hold back. He pushed into her one more time and lost it as his own orgasm pulsed through him, over him, around him. And the whole time, he held onto this slender woman, the only anchor in this chaotic world for the moment.

When he collapsed, he tried to move to the side of her, not wanting to crush her, but he wasn't sure he accomplished that objective. He smiled when she curled up against him though, enjoying the way she felt against his side. Another odd moment, he realized. Normally after sex he wanted to be gone. Once his body was satisfied, his mind instantly shifted back to business or issues of state. He honestly couldn't imagine moving a muscle right at this moment. And if Jalayla even attempted to move away from him, he would have to disabuse her of that notion. She was perfect right where she was.

Jalayla pushed her hair off of her shoulder, her mind still amazed at what she'd just experienced. And she couldn't stop touching him! What was it about this man that made her want to explore when she should be getting up and getting dressed?

But she couldn't stop. Her mouth kissed his chest, moving around and testing the taste and textures of various parts of his body. She smiled when she saw him harden once more and her curiosity could not be assuaged with a simple glance. She wanted to know more about this part of Tasir that gave her so much pleasure. Moving down to his stomach, she felt his muscles tighten. Looking up at his face, she smiled when she noticed that his eyes were still closed, one arm draped over his face even while his other hand continued to tangle in her hair, his fingers running through all the way to the ends.

Her mouth continued to move lower, her body shifting so that she was almost straddling him. The position was decadent and completely unladylike, but even that turned her on because it was so horribly against the rules she'd been brought up to obey. Everything about this day, this man, violated those rules. She'd never thought they were restrictive until she'd met this man and experienced the magic of his touch.

She moved lower, testing to see how far he would let her investigate. When he seemed to tense, his hand freezing in her hair for a moment, she took that to be an indication that he liked what she was doing. So she continued, moving lower, feeling her way with her fingers first then tasting with her lips and tongue. When she reached that mysterious part of him, she hesitated for only a moment before she wrapped her fingers around his hardness. It was fascinating! More interesting than she could have imagined! She'd always thought that this area on a male would be disgusting but she was wrong!

She let her fingers slide along the length of him, wondering if all men were this large. Jalayla was no longer reacting to his movements, she was focused only on her investigation of this solid flesh.

When she followed her previous pattern of fingers first, mouth second, she tasted tentatively at first. But when she heard the noises coming from him and looked up, she realized that he was enjoying this. Possibly just as much as she'd enjoyed what he'd done to her. When her mouth covered that part of him, he did the same thing she'd done, sat up and almost tried to get her off of him but when her tongue came into play, he fell back against the earth, enjoying her ministrations.

But not for long. She only had a few minutes of that excitement before he sat up again, lifting her off of him and settling her back down, but this time, impaled on that part of him that she loved so much.

Jalayla hadn't realized how turned on she'd become but his entry was soothed by the wetness of her own body and she thrilled to his invasion, her back arching so that her body could take him deeper. When his hands moved to her hips, lifting her up and showing her how to move, she was a quick student. And she loved this position! She could move against him, finding the ways that gave her the most pleasure. This was amazing, she thought, closing her eyes, her palms splayed out against his stomach as she moved up and down against him, feeling free to move however she liked.

But then his own hands moved up to cup her breasts, his thumbs teasing her nipples, both of them at the same time. No longer was there an enjoyable pleasure. When his forefingers came into play as well, the feelings that had been tingling inside of her roared to life. This was no longer pleasant, this was urgent! This was a desperate sensation to find that release, to achieve it so that this aching would go away. She whimpered as she moved, shifting frantically. His fingers were making her crazed and she couldn't...maybe...She tried to knock his hands away from her breasts, but he wasn't moving. And with a final tweak, that action took her over the edge, her body convulsing around his as she screamed.

Tasir watched, fascinated as she took pleasure from his body. But when she screamed out, she took him right along with him. He hadn't been expecting that but he'd known he was close. Watching her, feeling her nipples with his hands and feeling her body shudder almost violently with her climax, he was brought over the cliff so suddenly he could barely breathe for several moments.

He felt her collapse against his chest, her delectable body splayed out against him in the most erotic way. And he loved it! He tried to lift his arms to wrap around her, to hold her in place, but that climax had taken everything out of him. Never had he felt so replete!

It took a long time for both of them to get their breathing back to normal. When Tasir thought he could, he sat up, still with her intimately connected to him, and kissed her. His hands dove into her thick, dark hair and tilted her head so that he could deepen the kiss.

When he lifted his head, he looked down at the woman and a sense of possessiveness hit him hard.

Jalayla saw the look and turned shy, not sure what he was thinking. She didn't have long to wonder though. "How do you know about this place?" he asked her gently. She told him about her excursions here with Ciara over the years, all of the fun adventures the two of them had gotten into. He laughed and they talked of their childhoods, their new responsibilities, what they wanted for each of their countries, their lives…they talked until the sun started setting and a chill crept into the air.

She didn't want this time to end, but she couldn't think of any way to make it last longer. "I guess I'd better get dressed and head back to the fortress. I'm sure our fathers are wondering where we are."

He not only helped her stand up, he then lifted her into his arms and carried her into the water, rinsing off the remnants of their lovemaking in the cool water.

When they were once again standing on the edge of the water, pulling on their clothes despite their damp bodies, he looked down at her, his body once again ready to make love to her. He'd always had a strong sex drive, but there was something about this woman that was somehow different, and he wasn't sure he could get enough of her. There was only one solution.

"We'll tell our fathers that we plan to be married. And a short engagement," he stated firmly.

Jalayla looked up at him and froze in the process of putting her boots on. "Excuse me?" she replied. Her whole body was tense as she waited for him to correct his declaration.

And that's when it hit her. She remembered how arrogant and obnoxious this man was. Yes, he could be a fabulous lover, and when he wasn't being a bully, he was a nice guy and a great conversationalist. But deep down inside, she suspected that he really was too domineering for her taste.

He turned at the question, not sure why there would be any reason to hold back. "We'll talk to our fathers, let them know that we will be married."

She blinked as she stared up at him. "But we won't. Be married, that is," she countered, her fingers buttoning her shirt.

Jalayla started walking over to her horse which was still happily chomping on green wherever he could find it. But when she'd only taken a few steps, she felt his strong hand on her arm as he swung her back to face him. "What the hell are you talking about?" he demanded, furious that she would walk away from him and doubly angry that she wasn't agreeing to marry him. Women had been trying to manipulate him into marriage for years. Why would this tiny woman balk at the idea of marriage? And dammit, she was not going into the arms of another man! She was his woman! Hadn't he just proven that on the ground only a couple of hours ago?

Jalayla shrugged and walked over to her horse. "We had sex, Tasir. It doesn't require us to get married. Why would we ruin our lives by doing that? We'd hate each other before the first year passed."

His mind whipped back to their conversation, thinking that even that was stimulating. No way was he letting this woman get away from him! "You will marry me, Jalayla," he commanded even as he watched her get onto her horse. And yes, his body hardened once again as he admired the skill with which she controlled her mount.

"We will not be married, Tasir," she said as she turned her horse to face him. "We made a mistake here this afternoon. We shouldn't compound that mistake by getting married."

And with that, she turned and trotted down the barely-there pathway towards the fortress. She would pack her bags and get away before Tasir came back. She definitely didn't want to run into an angry Tasir again. He'd looked livid a moment ago.

But she still couldn't ignore the amazing feeling she had as she rode up to the fortress stables. And to be fair, that feeling was all because of his lovemaking. If there was any way to be married to the man but keep him from speaking, from ruining that amazing sense of well-being after their sexual interactions, she might consider marriage to him. Unfortunately, enjoying being in his arms was no reason to get married.

Okay, so yes, they'd had a very interesting conversation. But when it came right back down to the real world, he'd reverted right back to being a domineering, arrogant bully.

A few hours later, she still hadn't been able to locate her father. She was packed up and ready to leave, but she needed to explain to him what was going on, to give him an explanation for why she had to leave in a hurry. And every moment that it took her to locate him meant that there was a larger chance that she might run into Tasir.

Just like this morning, she meant to avoid him. The more she thought about this afternoon, the angrier she became. How dare he simply declare that they would be married! Who did he think he was? He definitely wasn't her father! He was only her lover! And no longer even that!

She was practically stomping into one of the salons as she thought about his obnoxious declaration while they were getting dressed. She had been told that her father was entertaining someone in this room but, once again, he was no longer here. There was evidence that he had been here at one point but no longer.

"I've been looking for you!" Tasir growled as he walked into the salon, closing the door behind him. "What the hell did you mean about us not getting married?"

Jalayla swung around, her eyes wide as she watched the man approach. She had her hands behind her back as she leaned against the table, her eyes looking into those of a very angry, very frustrated man. "I didn't think that needed any clarification, Tasir."

He towered over her, looking down into her nervous, brown eyes. "You were a virgin. We're getting married."

Her mouth fell open for a moment before she could close it again. "You want to marry me simply because you were my first lover?"

His jaw clenched at her question. "I will be your only lover, Jalayla. Get that through your pretty head."

She shook her head at his stubborn and unreasonable declaration. Of course, if he wanted to marry her for other....no, there was no reason for the two of them to ever be alone together. She just had to get away from him before her confused mind started to convince herself that she had feelings for this man. Because she didn't! They were good in bed together. That's it! "You're too domineering to even understand why we can't marry each other!" she came right back.

33

He shook his head and a slow smiled formed on those normally hard lips. "You like being dominated. Want me to prove it?"

Her eyes widened and she felt her body tighten with his words. Did she like it? Well, she'd definitely liked everything he'd done to her earlier today. And if she were honest with herself, she'd been pretty enthralled with the way he'd touched her last night. But did she like his overbearing manner? Maybe she just liked his experience, she cautioned herself.

She glanced to her left, but he was already anticipating her attempt to escape and he whipped an arm around her waist. "Not going to happen, princess," he said and lifted her up onto the table she'd been holding onto. He quickly slid her demure skirt up on her legs as he spread her knees and pressed his hips between her legs. He heard her gasp and looked down, noticing that her nipples were hard and peaked, pressing against the silk of her blouse. "I could take you right now," he growled as his teeth gently bit her ear lobe.

She liked the thought of that! How was that possible? She was a strong, confident woman and yet, here she was, breathing hard because this man was looming over her, the promise of that amazing release so temptingly close.

"No!" she countered, trying very hard to fight the pull of his body. She kept her hands flat on the table, her face turned away. But her head tilted, giving him more access to her neck. And of course, he took advantage of that.

His hands were already sliding up her legs, setting off all of those tingling sensations. "Tell me to stop," he coaxed but he bit her shoulder right at the edge of her sleeveless top, soothing it with his tongue and lips afterwards. "Tell me you don't like this."

His hands moved up underneath her blouse to cup her breasts and he pushed her shoulders back slightly so that she had to put her hands behind her or fall backwards. When his fingers slipped underneath her bra, his fingers teased her nipples. "You don't like this, do you?"

She trembled, her legs opening wider for him, that ache starting up again. "I don't like you," she corrected.

He chuckled softly against her ear. "Yes you do," he argued. "You love arguing with me, like we did last night." His fingers moved down her stomach, "Right before you came apart in my arms." And his hands moved up her thighs, his fingers hesitating at the lace edge of her underwear. "Tell me to stop and I will."

She felt his hands move away and grabbed his wrist, her eyes begging him to keep going. He'd gotten her to the point of no return in only minutes and she thought she might just melt into a puddle of need if he stopped now.

His eyes showed his triumph but his hands came back to her legs. "Put your hands behind your back," he commanded.

She hesitated and he pulled his hands away. When she realized what he was going to do, she quickly pressed her palms onto the polished wood of the table behind her. "Please," she begged, her knees lifting up to more perfectly cradle his hips.

"Don't you ever tell me you don't like this, Jalayla," he told her with a harsh whisper. "You were made for me and I can't get enough of you." With those words, her lace underwear was ripped apart and he stuffed the material into his pocket. She whimpered when his hands weren't touching her but he was quick to move them back. But he teased her, his movements soft and light when she needed firm action.

Her head fell back against her shoulders when she felt his fingers move inside of her. Just one at first, but then she felt the second one slip in and she inhaled, trying to make room for his long fingers.

"Say my name, Jalayla," he commanded.

She opened her mouth but when she hesitated, his fingers stopped moving. Her eyes flew open and she almost yelled, "Tasir! Your name is Tasir!"

With that, his fingers moved again, his thumb coming into play and her head fell backwards again.

With deft movements, Tasir unzipped his pants and slid his erection in where his fingers had just been, his eyes closing as her heat enveloped him. Slowly, he filled her up, watching her face to make sure he didn't hurt her. He'd been pretty rough earlier today and he was worried about her tender tissues. But she didn't seem to be too tender. In fact, she lifted her legs up, taking him deeper into her body. His hands grabbed her hips and pulled her closer to the edge of the table. "Lay back against the wood, Jalayla," he commanded.

She immediately followed his order and was rewarded by him moving against her, in and out, his body giving hers exactly what she wanted, what she needed. He felt the tension in her and knew what she was trying to do, to hold back and not give in to the amazing feelings but he wasn't going to allow that. His hand moved from between her breasts, still covered with silk, down over her soft stomach until he reached that bundle of nerves. With barely a touch, she splintered apart and he quickly followed, feeling it all the way down to his toes.

They stayed like that for a long time, both of them breathing heavily as they stared into each other's eyes. She smiled, her hand coming up to touch his jaw and he smiled back at her before turning to nip at her fingertips. "You're beautiful," he told her.

Jalayla laughed softly. "I'm a mess," she countered.

He shook his head, but as he did that, his eyes caught on the sunlight coming in from the window behind her. It suddenly occurred to him where they were and what they'd just done. He hadn't even locked the door!

She heard him mumble something under his breath and a moment later, he was gently lifting her up to a sitting position once again. Jalayla looked around, her eyes focusing once again and she realized where they were, that someone could have walked in on them at any point.

"Good grief!" she gasped and stepped back from him, straightening her clothes quickly. "Give me back my underwear," she hissed as she tucked her silk blouse back into her skirt.

"No," he replied and moved closer, hindering her efforts to present a calm and sophisticated front.

"What are you doing?" she tried to step back but he only pulled her closer by wrapping his arms around her waist.

"You say you don't like being dominated."

She glared up at him, her palms laying flat against his chest. "You're right. I don't."

"Okay, then come to my room tonight. You can be in charge." He bent down lower and looked into her brown eyes. "And in the end, you're going to admit the truth, understand?"

She had been trying to wiggle out of his arms but when he threw out that tantalizing offer, she stopped and looked up into his darker eyes. "I can be in charge?" she asked, her voice barely above a whisper as she thought about all the things she would like to do to him. Just like down at the creek, she could have the freedom to explore, to tantalize to her heart's content?

"After dinner," he told her, bending down and kissing her hard. "Come to my room. You know the way."

With that, he walked out of the salon, leaving Jalayla to stare at the open door but she didn't really see anything. She was so intrigued by the suggestion that she could barely think about anything else for the rest of the day. She didn't unpack, but neither did she find her father and tell him that she was leaving.

Dressing carefully for dinner that night, she chose a simple cocktail dress instead of a longer, more formal outfit. And she only put on diamond earrings, trying to keep things unfussy. Her black dress was made of silk, which added a bit of a sheen to the outfit, and she wore a pair of heels that gave her confidence as well as a bit more height.

She wanted to look sophisticated and elegant. Definitely not like she was anticipating a night of wickedness in a man's bed. But the moment she stepped into the drawing room where her father, Tasir and Tasir's father were having a pre-dinner drink, she knew that she wasn't going to be able to pull it off. As soon as she looked up into Tasir's dark eyes, she could feel her cheeks turning pink. She wasn't even sure if the blush was caused by anticipation for the night to come, or embarrassment at all that they had done earlier in the day.

And her discomfiture was made even more pronounced when he looked down at her, even while he was flanked by her father and his, and had the audacity to wink at her! The damned man knew how much she was anticipating tonight!

It didn't matter. She couldn't even rouse up a bit of anger at his wicked glances. She was just too excited.

And dinner lasted forever! There was a long, drawn out and almost angry discussion about some sort of shipping contract that the older men were arguing about. She didn't understand most of it, but it sounded like a simple solution would be to compromise on the shipping routes although neither parent was willing to do so. It was an odd conversation and one in which neither Tasir nor she participated.

When the main course was taken away by the ever-efficient servants, she excused herself, saying she was exhausted from the day.

The men all stood as she walked out but she only felt Tasir's eyes on her back. She carefully closed the doors to the dining room and made her way to her own room. Once there, she slid out of the dress and pulled on another silk nightgown. None of her nightwear was of the flirtatious style, but she had several that made her feel pretty. And he hadn't seemed to mind what she was wearing last night.

But when she'd finally dressed and was pacing her room, she wondered what in the world she was doing! She looked down at herself, clad only in a thin, silk nightgown and her body obviously was primed for yet another sexual encounter with Tasir.

She pushed her hair back off of her head, trying to get a grip on what she was planning, what she anticipated. How crazy was she? She should have just left this afternoon and sent her father a message. She was absolutely not going to do this tonight!

She paced back and forth, her brain telling her to stop thinking about going to his room tonight, to simply go to sleep and forget about the whole challenge. But her body wasn't going to allow her ignore the pull of the dare.

It was almost eleven o'clock when she sighed and sat down on her bed. Did she want to do this? Yes. Was it a horrible idea? Absolutely! Was she going anyway?

Yes.

She stood up and took a deep, calming breath. Once she saw him, she wouldn't be this nervous. Right?

She slipped through the secret hallway, her hand shaking as it held the flashlight. With each step, she told herself to go back, to run away and ignore the pull that was Tasir. But she didn't follow her brain's orders. When she felt the click on the door to his room, she took a deep breath and slipped through.

She found him pacing back and forth, wearing a pair of jeans that rode very low on his hips. When he saw her, his eyes widened slightly.

"You didn't know about the secret passageways?" she asked, leaning against the door. Almost as if she weren't fully committed to being here.

"I knew about them. It was why I told you to come through them. I just didn't think you'd come tonight."

She leaned against the secret door, her body shivering with nerves and anticipation. "Your offer was a bit too compelling," she finally told him. Her eyes drifted down, skimming across his chest and he smiled, eager for whatever she might be doing to him tonight.

He didn't move, just stood there, waiting for her.

"What do I do?" she finally asked.

He shrugged one of those massive shoulders. "You tell me," he dared her. "You're in charge, princess."

She smiled as she licked her lips. "Totally in charge?" she asked, stepping away from the secret doorway.

"Completely in charge," he assured her. "Just tell me what you want me to do."

She stepped closer, not really sure what she wanted. Except to touch him, she thought. Moving across the floor on almost silent feet, she stepped closer to him, her hands moving to his chest. "I can touch you all I want?"

"And anywhere you want," he assured her, looking down at her and his body was instantly hard and aching. That look in her eyes told him that she was extremely turned on by the idea and he loved this about her. He instantly knew that he was in trouble…and was going to love every moment of it.

When her soft fingers first touched his chest, he grunted as if he were in pain. And, in a way, he was in pain. He wanted to lift her up into his arms and carry her over to his bed. Every instinct within him wanted to take charge, to make love to her until she was screaming out his name.

But he wanted all of her. Including her admission that she liked what they did to each other. If he could get her to admit that, he suspected he might get her agreement to marry him. Why this was so important, he wasn't even thinking about. All he knew was that he wanted her. Forever!

Jalayla ran her fingers over every inch of his chest, her fingers sliding against the textured skin that was so different from her own. She was fascinated by his skin that was so much darker than hers. When her fingers slid over his flat, male nipple, she heard him hiss through his teeth and she liked that sound. So she did it again, garnering the same results. Remembering the way he'd tortured her breasts earlier today, she moved her head closer, her lips capturing his nipple and tormenting it mercilessly.

When she felt his hands on her hips, she looked up at him, trying to be stern. "Take your hands off of me," she told him.

He stared at her for a long moment, considering just ignoring her order. But in the end, he reminded himself of the long-term goal and his hands slid off of her hips, hanging next to his hips.

Jalayla smiled and went back to her exploration. She moved over his chest and stomach, stopping when she reached the waistband of his jeans. Her fingers slid underneath the material as if she were about to unsnap, but when she felt his stomach muscles tighten, she pulled back and moved around to the back of him. She gave the muscles in his back equal time and found several spots that were almost as reactive as the front of him.

When she came back around to the front, she wanted very badly for him to lift her up into his arms and carry her over to the enormous bed, to make love to her like he had earlier this morning. But she remembered that she was in charge and bit her lower lip. "Take off your jeans and go lie down," she told him.

His jeans were gone swiftly and he wasn't wearing anything else underneath. When he walked stiffly over to the bed, he laid on his back, his feet on the floor. "Now what, princess?" he asked, his eyes almost taunting her.

She climbed onto the mattress and looked down at him, her mouth watering at all of the ideas running through her mind. But instead of acting on any of them, she stood up and slid her nightgown off of herself. She smiled when Tasir lifted his head up, his dark eyes taking in her now-naked body. She wasn't aware of how his eyes followed her because she was too intent on following him down onto the bed. She was still shy, but fighting that part of herself. As she sat down beside him, her hands moved to cover her breasts.

"You can't do that," he cautioned her.

Jalayla looked up, startled.

"Cover yourself," he said, nodding to her arms that were crossed over her chest. "If you're in charge, you have to be sure of yourself."

She shook her head, unaware of the way her dark hair drifted over her shoulders. "I can do whatever I want," she came right back. "I'm in charge, right?"

He sighed and leaned back down. "Okay, so what's your next step?" he teased, enjoying her excitement even if this was moving too slowly for his taste.

She looked up and down his body, not sure what she wanted to do. So she simply leaned down and started the same process she'd done earlier today but this time, she kept her hands on his wrists, refusing to let him touch her for fear that he would stop her again.

She kissed him and enjoyed experimenting, tasting and feeling him against her skin.

She almost laughed out loud with delight when she heard him moan. "Jalayla, I can't take much more," he told her, his voice sounding harsh. She looked up and realized that he was still laying on his back but his body was rigid, sweat breaking out on his forehead as he tried to control himself.

She took pity on him and moved higher up on his body. When she was straddling him once again, she took him into her body, feeling all of him inside of her and loving it. "Okay, I'm releasing control. Please..." she started to say something but she was flipped over onto her back and he was pressing himself into her. It was so powerful, she screamed out, her body arching up into his. It didn't take long before she was splintering apart and his climax quickly followed.

She was still breathing heavily when he pulled her higher up onto the bed, his arm curling around her as he pulled her closer against him. He tried to form words, but nothing would come out. A few moments later, he felt her breathing settle down and he knew that she was asleep.

Unwilling to be separated from her for even a moment, he reached out with his arm and turned off the light. He'd have to wake her before dawn so that she could go back to her own room, but until then, she was his. And he would keep her close to him for as long as he possibly could.

Chapter 4

Jalayla watched Tasir breathe in and out, admiring his astonishing chest, all those delicious muscles as well as the way his long lashes looked against his tanned skin. He really was an amazingly handsome man, she thought. All arrogance aside, he was a good man. And while he was sleeping, she could admit that she liked him. Well, more than liked him. She felt something for the man that…it didn't make sense. She'd known him for too short a time and…Jalayla shook her head. Her feelings didn't make sense. They were too strong, too…she didn't want to feel this way towards Tasir.

It was too bad that she would have to leave. She wanted nothing more than to crawl back into bed and curl up against him once more.

But it was time, she knew. It was time to head home, to face reality.

Their time together had been nothing more than a dare, a time where they explored each other's bodies. He taught her about sensuality and she taught him…well, perhaps she'd taught him a few manners along the way. She wasn't completely sure of that, but it made her feel better to think it was true.

She jerked out of her reverie when Tasir rolled over, his arm reaching out, obviously looking for her. Jalayla knew she had to hurry. He'd woken her up several times last night, making love to her and then, after their bodies were sated once again, talking about their lives and what they wanted for each of their countries. They even discussed the unexplainable increasing tensions between their countries which had been allies for so long. Neither of them understood what was going on or why there was so much unrest. But they both wanted to do what they could to ease the tensions.

As she slipped through the secret door and made her way back to her room, she thought that it was almost as if they were both thinking the same way, wanting the same things for their countries and willing to do whatever they could to make their countries better.

Unfortunately, their time together was not permanent. They'd both known that going into this affair. She'd understood the parameters of their relationship before she'd even left her room last night.

Now she had to face the world – although she would do it with different eyes. Tasir might have only made love to her, but she felt different. The world felt different this morning.

She slipped into the dining room and caught her father just as he was finishing up his breakfast. "We're leaving, my dear," he said and wiped his mouth with a napkin.

"I suspected as much," she said as she poured herself a cup of coffee. She couldn't eat breakfast since her stomach was in knots. She didn't want to leave Tasir, but she knew that he had things he had to do, responsibilities that didn't include her. "I'm already packed."

Her father nodded and she thought that he looked angry for some reason. "Is everything okay?" she asked, laying a hand on his arm.

He sighed and patted her hand. "Yes. Things just didn't go as smoothly this week as I'd hoped. We were supposed to stay for further discussions." He shook his head and started to say something but stopped himself. "Something is wrong, Jalayla. And the tensions are not getting better."

Her eyes widened slightly. "Are you talking about the attacks in the south?

He nodded his head, his expression grim. "There is evidence that," his eyes glanced to the right and left, worried that they might be overheard. "Well, that the violence is escalating and it is coming from either Lurasa or Altair. We're not exactly sure. We're still sifting through the information."

Jalayla shivered. "It wasn't from Lurasa," she told him, sure about that after her late night conversations with Tasir.

Her father's eyes swiveled around to her. "How do you know?"

She shrugged, looking down at her hands because she wasn't able to look her father in the eyes. "I've been talking with Prince Tasir. And I know that he's just as confounded as you are."

He sighed and rubbed the back of his neck. "Then his father is telling the truth," he said and his shoulders seemed tense. "Let's go home, my dear. Maybe there is more information that we can look at that will make this whole problem seem sensible."

An hour later, she walked out on his arm, her eyes searching the hallways for one more look at Tasir. She wanted to say goodbye to him, but she wasn't sure if she should. Maybe it was better to just leave, to end the short-lived relationship quickly. Sort of like ripping off a Band-Aid. Better to do it fast, with just a little pain than to make it go on and on.

So she walked out of the Fortress of the Guards behind her father, stepping into the armored limousine and wishing that things could be different. Wouldn't it be wonderful if the marriage she'd been dreading for so long could be with Tasir instead of some unknown stranger?

Such was not her lot in life, she reminded herself as the vehicle pulled away, heading back out of the fortress towards home.

Chapter 5

Jalayla pushed herself up off of the toilet, grabbing a washcloth and trying to cool off her cheeks. This nausea was…terrifying! Every morning she felt horrible but, so far, she refused to contemplate the reason behind her morning need to rush to the bathroom.

When she felt somewhat human again, she grabbed her toothbrush and brushed her teeth, hoping that the minty taste might calm her stomach.

She'd been away from Tasir for six weeks now. Six long weeks of loneliness and avoiding his calls. Why answer them? There was nothing either of them could do!

Well, that's the way she'd thought about it for the previous five weeks. For the past five or six days, she'd started to consider other options.

A knock on the door startled her and she had to grab the edge of the countertop to try and keep her stomach settled. "Yes?" she called out, knowing it was her maid coming to check on her. She'd been doing that a lot lately.

"I'm sorry to disturb you, Your Highness," her maid called through the door, "But your father has requested your presence in his office."

Jalayla closed her eyes for a moment. "When?" she asked when she could form the words.

"He asked for you to come to him immediately."

Jalayla almost groaned out loud. Her father had been looking at her strangely lately. She knew what was going to happen and she didn't want to face that future! She just knew that he'd arranged her marriage. Maybe it was to that weak boy in Dubai, the one that used to sneeze a lot. Or perhaps her father wanted her marry her off to that irritating prince that lived in New York now. She couldn't even remember what country he was supposed to be from. Did it really matter?

She wanted to see Tasir! She wanted to feel his arms around her, to argue with him and defy him and laugh with him! She didn't want any of those annoying, weak and insipid boys that didn't know what being a man was all about. Tasir did! Tasir was the man she wanted.

Goodness, how her story had changed now that she'd been away from him for so long. She missed him terribly. Well, to be honest, she'd missed him horribly from the first moment they'd parted, but she'd cried herself to sleep at night, telling herself that it was for the best.

Now she wasn't so sure.

"My lady?" her maid called out again.

Jalayla realized she'd been sitting silently in the bathroom, contemplating how much she missed the man.

"I'll be right there," she called back.

Straightening once more, she smoothed her hair and her dress, took a deep breath, then stepped out of the bathroom. She smiled politely at her maid as she walked out of her room and made her way towards her father's office.

Maybe her father only wanted to see her because she'd been avoiding him more and more lately. If she didn't speak to him, she didn't have to hear about the man she'd have to spend the rest of her life with.

The guard outside her father's office opened the heavy wooden door immediately. Jalayla stepped inside, her knees shaking a bit as she approached his desk.

"You wanted to see me?" she asked, noticing how angry he looked all of a sudden.

Her father's bushy eyebrows were pressed low over his eyes and his lips were compressed as he watched her come closer. "What have you done?" he demanded.

Jalayla bowed her head. "I'm…"

He didn't want to hear her explanations because nothing could explain away her behavior. "You've ruined everything! Do you have any idea how your actions are going to affect this country? The people here love you! They will fight for your honor! And you've…"

How could her father know about her affair with Tasir and her pregnancy? Goodness, he was furious with her!

"That's enough!" a deep voice said from behind her.

Jalayla swung around, her hungry eyes searching for Tasir. Was he really here? When she spotted him, she didn't stop to think about anything. Her feet were moving before her brain cautioned her against the action. Within moments, her legs had carried her over to him and she flung herself into his arms. It wasn't until she was inches away from him that she remembered that she'd ignored so many of his calls and he might not feel the same way about her. But as his strong arms closed around her, she breathed much more easily.

"You are in so much trouble, woman," he whispered in her ear as he hugged her, squeezing her until he realized what he was doing and that he might hurt her.

"I can't believe you're here," she said, blinking hard to fight back the tears. "I'm so sorry that I didn't return your calls. I was being an idiot."

He pulled back, just enough so that he could look at her beautiful features. "Don't let it happen again," he told her, his hand coming up to cup her cheek, a thumb reaching out and capturing the tear that spilled over her dark lashes. "You have some explaining to do, my love."

She laughed at his tenderness because she knew that it was reserved only for her. "I know."

"Just tell me you love me and it will all be worth it."

She laughed again, dropping her head against his chest. "Arrogant to the last, aren't you?" she asked. "But yes. I love you. And I can't believe how much I missed you."

"I love you too. But we have a pretty big mess that we need to clear up."

Her smile brightened now that she was back in his arms. "Anything can be fixed now. I can't believe I left that morning. I never should have gone back to my room." She wrapped her arms around his lean waist, reveling in how good he felt. And smelled! Oh my how she loved the way he smelled! It was all man, all Tasir!

"Jalayla!" she heard her father snap behind her.

She swung around, but Tasir kept her pinned against his side, not letting her move away from him.

"Sorry, Father," she said but kept her arm around his waist as well. "I guess there are a lot of things I need to explain."

Her father's furious eyes glanced between the two of them. "I believe this man has explained a great deal, just by showing up. What I'd like to know is how you so completely lost your sense of who you are and the responsibilities you have to Tularia to allow any of this to happen!"

Jalayla cringed, never having seen her father this angry before. And he didn't even know all of it. She hadn't told anyone that she was pregnant and she was fairly certain that her father didn't know all that she and Tasir had done at the fortress. He only knew that she loved Tasir. Nothing more though. At least, she hoped that was all he knew. "I'm not sure I can really explain it either." She glanced up at the man she loved so much. "When I first met him, I thought he was the worst sort of man. But as I got to know him, I…"

When she couldn't finish, Tasir stepped in. "It's my fault, Your Highness. She behaved with complete dignity and I'm the one who acted inappropriately."

Jalayla's father rolled his eyes. "I doubt it. I know my daughter too well. She probably…" he threw his hands up in the air. "It doesn't matter. What's done is done. We'll just…" He rubbed the space between his eyes as if he were trying to fight off a headache.

Tasir stepped into the silence. "The contracts will have to be destroyed."

Jalayla looked up at him, not sure what was going on. He turned back to her and explained, "My father arranged for me to marry Princess Ciara."

Jalayla couldn't believe the stab of jealousy she felt that her friend might be marrying this man. "No!"

"And you're supposed to be marrying Prince Zoran next month," he continued.

She pulled back a bit more, confused now. "And yet…." Her hand fluttered to her stomach unconsciously. She couldn't say a word about the pregnancy now. In fact, she was more confused at this moment than she was before she'd walked in here. What was going on? A marriage contract that her father hadn't spoken to her about? How could he have done something like that? They always talked about important issues and she'd known that she would have to marry in a political union.

Tasir saw the confusion and panic in her eyes and tried to reassure her. "I know. It's all a horrible mix-up. The problem is more about how the people will perceive this rather than anything else. There won't be any hard feelings involved from our end." He turned to Jalayla's father. "We can work out the details."

Jalayla turned to look at her father. He suddenly seemed older than his years. "The contracts are all set in place. The negotiations have been finalized."

Tasir's arm tightened on Jalayla's waist. "Then we'll have to renegotiate. It won't be the first time a contract has been set aside when new facts were discovered. Besides, a union with Lurasa would be much more beneficial to your country than one with Larcatia. There are significant benefits that need to be examined, Your Highness."

Jalayla stepped into the conversation, citing all of the issues between the four countries and why it would be better to be aligned with Lurasa versus Larcatia. They all sat down together, keeping the sheik's advisors out of the conversation. This was just between the three of them for now.

Tasir conferenced in his father, who had already been apprised of the situation. Between the four of them, they all agreed to broach the possibility of canceling the arranged marriages with Larcatia and Altair.

"But it will have to be done carefully," Jalayla's father cautioned at the end of the discussion. "And you have to leave. There can be no hint of this until it is a done deal," he told Tasir.

As much as he wanted to argue about it, Tasir knew that her father was right. He looked down at Jalayla. "Are you going to be okay?" he asked her gently.

She smiled up at him, all the love she felt for this man shining through in her eyes. "Absolutely. Just get the discussions moving quickly."

Her father nodded. "We can start the conversations next week. I believe Princess Ciara is out of the country anyway, so she hasn't been told about the marriage contract. And Prince Zoran," her father sighed. "Well, thankfully, he's on his annual hiking vacation." He shook his head. "The man goes out into the woods for a week every year. Each time I hear about it, I always think it is crazy. But at this point in time, I would love to change places with him." Her father was walking out of his office. "I'd rather be anywhere than here," he said and left them alone.

Jalayla turned when the door to her father's office door closed, looking up at Tasir. "Thank you for coming for me," she whispered, overawed by his tenacity.

He pulled her closer. "Never doubt the extent of my arrogance," he teased.

She laughed and laid her head against his muscular chest. "I never did," she came right back. "It's that arrogance that is going to give us our happily ever after."

He kissed her then. "I have to go. I'll get with Zoran as soon as he's back from the woods. He and I have been friends for a long time. I'm sure this can be worked out."

"I'll call Ciara as soon as I find out where she's gone. I know she probably doesn't want to marry you anyway. You're all mine."

News Flash: More tensions on the borders, a report said. The fighting is intensifying and villagers are starting to take sides.

News Flash: The annual festival celebrating the culture of the regions has been canceled. Officials cite rising levels of threats as well as lower interest. Suspicions between border villages are to blame.

News Flash: A large contingent of soldiers was seen on the southern border earlier tonight. The forces seem to be practicing but government officials are worried about the presence of military personnel so close to the border, which had previously been quiet.

Dancing with the Dangerous Prince: Chapter 1

Breathing slowly, heart pounding, feet moving, chilly, moist air whooshing past her face and arms to cool her off....this was the best time of the morning. Ciara felt her feet thump along the soft dirt, her body relishing the exercise of a good, long run. There was nothing better than a run through the woods to clear one's mind, get ready for the upcoming day. The pace wasn't always steady but this path she'd discovered never failed to make her body sing with the effort as she raced through the trees.

Whenever worries about the future, of what might happen when she had to leave this job at the end of the week started to filter into her mind, she pushed herself harder. This wasn't a time to worry about anything. This was her time to just be a part of nature, part of the world around her.

She was rounding a corner and saw the movement off in the distance, which was odd since normally, she was the only one out here this early. It was predawn and the horizon looked almost silvery as the sun started to break through the early morning haze.

The man she saw was...shocking! He was so impressive that she actually blinked, just to see if perhaps her mind was playing tricks on her. He literally stopped her in her tracks.

Whoa, she thought, seeing his arm and back muscles bulge as he pulled himself up the cliff's edge. Ciara watched as....

Where had that stump come from? Looking down, she quickly regained her footing then hurriedly glanced back up towards where she'd seen the man. He was gone!

Shoot, she thought. Her eyes scanned the horizon but nothing else moved. Where had he gone so quickly?

Picking up her pace once more, she ran her usual route along the lake but she had a hard time getting back into the rhythm. And it was all because of that man! He'd been absolutely divine! Never had she seen such a perfectly formed male specimen.

Perhaps she'd just imagined him. This was a pretty remote part of the woods. The summer camp where she worked was careful about the surrounding area, going on hikes only in groups because of the potential of wild animals. The kids were normally pretty loud, scaring off any bears or other animals, but one never knew and so the staff was always careful.

But this man was out there in the distance alone.

Shaking her head, thinking she had just imagined the man pulling himself up onto the cliff, she pushed herself harder, wanting to finish her run and shower before the summer camp kids woke up. As a camp counselor, it took a lot of energy and focus to keep the kids moving in the right direction and teach them everything that the brochure promised to the parents. Between the camping, swimming, archery, arts and crafts and all the other activities, her days were never boring.

Zoran stood on the cliff, looking down at the lake. The silence and stillness of the hazy morning soothed the bitter stress of the past year. Tensions were rising between his country and its neighbors, countries that had been friendly for decades. But out here with the trees and the mountains, the soothing lake and the rising sun, things were peaceful and calm. The world was kind and gentle when he looked out upon the valley. He had one week to himself each year and he needed to absorb as much of the calm as possible before heading back to his responsibilities.

The sudden figure of a slender woman running along the edge of the lake caught his eye. She was a good runner, strong and smooth, keeping a steady pace as she dashed in and out of his sight through the trees. He stood on the edge of the cliff watching her, fascinated by the steady fall of her feet against the earth. And her body. Yes, it was her body that had captured his attention. That long, dark ponytail smacking her back, her strong legs, arms and…she turned a corner in the trail and his eyes feasted on pert breasts and a slender waist. She was perfection, he thought. From this distance, he couldn't see her face, but he suspected that she would be lovely. Though he soon lost sight of her in the forest, her image continued to dwell in his mind throughout the day.

"Ciara, you've got drawing class today. Mike, you set up the swimming lessons. Joanna…." The camp director called out the various assignments to each of the counselors. Some of the instructors were hired for a specific camp activity such as lifeguard or cook. The rest of them, like her, were shuffled around as the day's focus changed. Today, art was the big thing. Puppet making, painting, drawing, wood carving…various art stations would be set up around the camp areas. All of the kids would rotate through each of the stations.

Twenty minutes later, her first group was trekking up the path into the woods, ready to learn how to draw. It was still a little chilly, but the sun would heat up the day and it would be steamy by the afternoon. Ciara didn't mind, though. She liked the heat. Thrived on it, actually. The earthy humidity she could do without, but just being outdoors, free from the normal stresses of her average day, was wonderful.

She looked around at the campers, understanding that drawing a bunch of trees might not be the most exciting station they would visit today, but she was going to make it as fun as possible. "Okay, so pick up your charcoal pencil and just draw whatever you see. It doesn't have to be perfect, it can just be interesting," she said. The kids each grabbed a drawing paper, clipboard, and a charcoal pencil, found a perch on a rock or a log, and started drawing the trees. Or each other, she noticed with amusement.

She wandered to each of the campers, giving them tips on how to draw or sometimes helping them decide what to draw when they seemed to be looking around in utter confusion. All the while, she encouraged each of them as she went.

It was when she reached one girl who was sitting a bit further out than the rest that she saw him again. Ciara was still facing the group but, as she glanced behind the rock where the girl was sitting, her eyes caught on…was that a naked man?

"Oh my," she breathed as she watched the seriously nude man dive into the water pouring down from a waterfall. The spot where he was diving wasn't very deep and she was pretty sure that the water would be cold at this point in the morning, but goodness, it didn't seem to affect him in any way. In a few hours, once the summer sun had warmed up the air, the cool water of the waterfall and stream would be perfect. But this early in the morning, she wouldn't relish such a dip into the cold water.

When he surfaced from his dive, his hand pushed his dark hair back and she felt faint. She realized she hadn't been breathing and took a large influx of oxygen as she continued to stare, mesmerized by the man and all of those amazing, delicious, bulging…muscles! He was lifting himself out of the pool and moving towards the waterfall that now splashed down onto a flat rock. She was only looking at his muscles, she promised herself but her eyes inadvertently drifted lower and she was…wow!

Their eyes clashed. He was still far enough away that she couldn't see details, but she felt the impact of that gaze like a sudden punch. It was like a laser beam of heat slicing through the cool mist of the morning, and she gripped the edge of the boulder underneath her hand as her body melted with his gaze.

He wouldn't release her, she thought. Not that she was trying very hard. She watched in utter fascination as he dove back into the water. Frustratingly, he was once again submerged and she continued to watch as his strong arms started moving, pushing through the stream to the edge of the water.

Before he started getting out again, he looked up at her, making sure she was still watching. Which, of course, she was! What woman in her right mind would be able to look away from such perfection? When he assured himself that she was watching, he started to lift himself up again, out of the water onto a rock along the edge.

He wasn't going to do it, she thought frantically. She would look away. She absolutely would not ogle the amazingly well-put-together stranger. But those eyes! They were daring her! Sure enough, he was getting out! He was slowly pulling himself out of the water.

Inch by inch, she watched as those shockingly huge arms lifted him out with agility. Just as he'd done this morning, those muscles bunched up and he easily stepped onto the rock at the water's edge.

Standing up, he proudly revealed himself to her. All naked male. Protruding parts looking more than impressive! Wasn't there some sort of joke about what cold water did to the male...physique? That must be untrue, because she knew that the stream water was cold and she now knew that this man's...physique...was definitely not affected by that cold water.

When he simply stood there, daring her to look at his body, she felt heat swamp over her. Her breasts felt heavy and every muscle in her body tightened. Low in her belly, she felt the impact of his nakedness and she had the crazy urge to move forward, to meet him so that she could touch as well as see.

"Ciara?" one of the campers called out.

Ciara jerked backwards, her eyes moving to her students who were all diligently drawing the trees and rocks. "Yes!" she gasped, shocked that she'd completely forgotten about all of her kids. She glanced back, just one more look. He was standing there, his hands on his hips, relaxed almost except for that...part...of him.

She shook her head, trying to regain her focus, and moved back around the rock where she couldn't succumb to temptation again. She was working! And with kids! Goodness, if any of those kids had seen that man, gloriously naked, it would be the talk of the camp for the next week!

"Okay, let's see what you've done!" she called out. The kids all looked up, probably because she sounded overly enthusiastic. Was her face red? Probably.

The next group of kids was walking up the pathway and she was relieved. Glancing behind her, she almost sobbed when she realized that the man was no longer there. Where had he gone? Was she upset that he was gone? Or relieved? She should be relieved, but the honest side of her accepted that she would definitely like another peek at that man. She'd never seen anyone as well put together as he was.

Zoran couldn't believe that a slip of a woman could have this much of an impact on him and she wasn't even touching him. He stood at the edge of the water, demanding that she look at him, not allowing her to even glance away.

He wanted her!

And he could tell by her body movements that she wanted him. From this distance, he could make out more details of her face. Those cat-like eyes fascinated him and he wanted to know what color they were. Her legs were long and muscular while her waist was tiny. He couldn't see enough of her breasts because of the loose shirt, and that irritated him. He'd seen those beauties while running earlier today and he felt cheated now because they weren't on display.

She moved away suddenly and he wanted the heat from her glance back on him. He felt angered by the fact that she'd disappeared.

He was going to find her. This was imperative, he realized.

Moving easily over the rocks, he grabbed his clothes and hiking boots. Dressing quickly, he stepped through the forest, his sense of direction leading him directly to her.

Ciara felt the hairs on the back of her neck lift, sensing danger. Looking around, her eyes scanned the trees for wild animals. When she didn't see anything initially, she glanced at the sky. The threat wasn't coming from the weather either. The sun was still shining, not a cloud in the sky.

She looked around again and that's when she saw him. He wasn't close, but he was closer than she'd seen him all day. He was perched on a rock, once again looking relaxed. Even as that thought occurred to her, she suspected that this man never relaxed. The look in his eyes shouted out "predator", but she didn't run. She stared for a long moment before one of the students asked her a question, bringing her attention back to her job. It took her several moments to understand the student's words, but she took a few deep breaths, trying to refocus her mind.

For the next hour, he sat there watching her, making her nervous but also…shockingly alive! There was something about this tall, muscular man with the dangerous eyes that called to her. Something that drew her closer, almost as if she were swimming around him in a circle, coming closer and closer but never too near for fear of being stung. That analogy didn't make any sense and she concentrated on showing one of the students how to draw branches more clearly. Ciara chided herself since she wasn't circling anyone and she definitely wasn't getting closer to that man. She kept looking in his direction to make sure he was still there and he hadn't gotten closer. But as the hour grew later, she realized that she wasn't worried about him coming closer. She was anxious about him leaving her again. He'd disappeared on her earlier today and she didn't want that to happen again.

Although, that begged the question – why not? If he was so dangerous, why didn't she want him to go? She should be hoping that he would disappear back into the deep woods and leave her safely tucked away in the summer camp perimeter.

When the last group of students made their way down the pathway, she stood there frozen in place, but every cell in her body seemed to be pinging around, alive and excited because she could feel him nearby. He hadn't left her! He hadn't disappeared! Ciara knew that she should follow her students, should run down the pathway to safety. It was time for dinner, she should be making her way down to the dining hall and helping with the dinner setup or ensure that the kids were cleaning up and heading towards the dining hall themselves.

But she didn't move. She couldn't move.

When the last of the campers turned the corner in the pathway, she spun around, intent on climbing up to where he was perched.

But as soon as she turned, he was there! Less than five feet away!

This stranger who had popped in and out of her day was no longer hiding. He was there! So close!

And goodness, he was taller and larger than she'd thought. She'd only seen him from a distance, but up close, he was more amazing than her imagination could have created. His eyes were dark and deep set while his cheekbones were more prominent and his jaw promised determination. The combination of the handsome, hard features and the rock hard body was… spellbinding!

"You're here," she whispered, her eyes traveling back up to his black gaze.

"You didn't leave," he came right back.

She wanted to glance back down the pathway, to make sure that none of the campers saw this man, but his eyes wouldn't let her look away.

"They're gone," he confirmed. Hazel, he realized. Her pretty, cat eyes were hazel. Almost green, but not quite. With a bit of yellow, making him think of dragon eyes. Soft, sweet, nervous dragon eyes. A contradiction, he thought.

How had he known what she was thinking? And more importantly, why was she standing here? Why was she not running away, back to safety? How many times had her father or her bodyguards warned her that strangers were to be avoided? Everything about this man screamed dangerous predator and the image of a rabbit popped into her mind. She was the rabbit and this man, with his dark eyes, black hair and his tanned skin holding in all those bulging muscles, was the ultimate predator.

"I won't hurt you," he promised.

She blinked, and tilted her head back slightly. "Stop doing that," she told him, wanting to back up but refusing to do it. She wouldn't show this man how scared she was. But was it fear? Or something else?

A dark eyebrow went up with her command. "Stop doing what?"

She swallowed, her tongue darting out to moisten her painfully dry lips. In the back of her mind, she heard the leaves rustling overhead, the birds chirping happily and, even farther away, the laughter from the summer camp. "Stop reading my mind."

He smiled slightly and those marvelous muscles in his arms tightened even more. "I'm not reading your mind. Your eyes were about to dart away from me. You're a camp counselor. It stands to reason that you were trying to ensure the safety of your charges."

Slowly, her head nodded. She was still impressed even though the things he'd said were probably pretty basic assumptions on his part.

His eyes moved down her figure, clad in shorts and a tee-shirt. "And you're a small woman. I'm a stranger significantly larger than you are. It stands to reason that, when I move closer, you would want to run away."

She thought about that, her eyes moving down his magnificent body. He was wearing a brown tee-shirt, but the material in no way hid the muscles that were underneath. In fact, the fabric strained to contain all of those captivating muscles.

"I don't." She suspected she should clarify, explain that she didn't want to run away. But when his eyes looked back into hers, she realized that he'd understood perfectly.

He looked down, his eyes focusing on her lips. "Good. I won't hurt you."

Her lips quirked up into a smile. "Said every serial killer," she teased.

His eyes reflected her laughter. "Good point. Who are you?"

"Ciara," she told him, not bothering with her last name because it required too much effort.

"Zoran."

"Very pleased to meet you Zoran." In the distance, she heard the dinner bell ring. "I have to go." She immediately started to move away, but when she felt his rough fingers touch her arm gently, she stopped and looked back up at him, startled by his touch.

"Come back after dinner," he commanded.

Ciara was tempted, but she shook her head. "I can't."

"You're afraid of me," he stated with rising frustration because, for the first time, a woman fascinated him and he wasn't sure how to approach her without terrifying her. He didn't want her to leave. He needed to see her, to touch her. Hell, right at this moment, with those perfect, full breasts pressing their pointed nipples against her tee-shirt, he wanted to devour her. He didn't think she would appreciate the intensity of that need at the moment.

Ciara took a deep breath and looked back up into the coal-dark depths of those eyes. "Should I be?"

Zoran thought about it for a long moment, tried to put himself in her shoes. With all of the news reports of women putting themselves in danger, he could understand why she should run far and fast away from him. He nodded slowly. "Probably."

His honesty was refreshing and, despite the fact that he was telling her she was probably better off never seeing him again, she actually felt safer. Laughing, she relaxed ever so slightly. "Thanks for the warning." Unfortunately, the bell chimed again. "I really have to go."

She was just about to turn around and head down the pathway when his words stopped her again. "Do you always do what you're told?"

She smiled because, yes, she did. Her father was quite dictatorial – although she knew that he loved her very much. "Yes," she finally said, turning to head towards the pathway again. Her forward momentum was stopped though, when he said, "Good."

She glanced back at him, her startled eyes taking in his large form and the change in his tension.

She wasn't sure what to do. She desperately wanted to stay, to get to know this man, but she had responsibilities in the camp and she didn't want to put herself in danger by remaining in the woods with a man she didn't know. Goodness, her guards would be furious with her just for the short period of time she'd already spent in his company. And her father would be livid at all she'd seen of him earlier this morning!

"Come back. I won't touch you. I just want to talk to you, Ciara."

She heard his words and a part of her was disappointed. She wanted so much more than talking, but she wasn't sure what that was.

Zoran saw the look in her eyes and his body reacted. He had a critical need to connect with this beauty, wanting to possess her in the most elemental way. But he also realized that he was scaring her. That look, that need was there in her eyes as well but she was banking it, suppressing it because this was a crazy situation. Never would he have thought he would find a woman like her in the woods. "Come back here after dinner. Or whenever you're off duty."

She smiled softly, feeling wanted. His eyes screamed out his desire for her and she liked it. "I'll be back in an hour."

He nodded his head. "I'll be here."

She turned and almost ran down the pathway, nervous once again, but for a whole different reason.

Dinner with the campers and counselors that night seemed to go on forever! She kept glancing at the clock, trying to figure out when she would be off duty. When the kids finally started their cleanup duties, she practically jumped out of her chair to help them, wanting the process to move more quickly. There was a campfire each night where the kids would sing songs or tell stories. Sometimes they put on a skit. But she wasn't required to be there for that. As soon as the dining hall was cleaned up and emptied, she was off duty for the day.

When the gong finally sounded for the campfire to start, she herded the kids out to the wooden benches, but stood off to the back, not wanting to become a part of tonight's activities. The other staffers who weren't on duty slowly faded backwards as well. Many of them would congregate back in the kitchen, chatting over a final cup of coffee. And normally, she would join them.

She looked at the kids, happily singing along with the camp fire songs, then back at the dining hall where the other staffers that were off duty were already migrating. She wasn't going to the dining hall tonight. She watched until the door to the hall closed and then she slowly backed away from the fire light. When she reached the darkness, she was gripping her flashlight tightly, more than ready to slip into the night and find her stranger-man.

She didn't have far to look. She was on her way back up the pathway when she spotted him, feeling nervous about the enigmatic combination of nocturnal stillness and intermittent sound. He wasn't at the top of the pathway this time. In fact, he was right at the edge of the woods, waiting for her.

He held out his hand for her and she hesitated for only a moment. Putting her hand into his, she almost jerked it right back out, startled by the heat of his touch. At the first sign of her reluctance, he tightened his fingers reassuringly and pulled her closer.

"Don't be afraid of me, Ciara," he coaxed softly so that no one else could hear them. "I promise I won't hurt you."

Her breathing increased and she looked up at him, wishing she could see his face. There was so little light here and she wanted, needed, to see his eyes. She opened her mouth to say something, but the words wouldn't come out. It was almost as if she were hypnotized by this man, the mysterious quiet of the night and the cocooning nature of the darkness.

"How about if we just sit here and talk?" he offered.

She breathed a sigh of relief. "That would be good," she replied, finding a moss covered log to perch on. She then sat there awkwardly, not really sure what to talk about. This man didn't seem like the type that would want to trade shopping stories, not that she shopped all that much either.

"Tell me about what you do at the camp," he asked, trying to help her relax and show her that he wasn't a threat.

They talked for hours, she realized later. Not about anything in particular, but just the sort of conversation that two people have when they're getting to know each other. She hadn't realized how much time had passed until she was laughing about something he said and her eyes flashed over to the camp grounds. It was almost completely dark!

"Oh my goodness," she said, jumping up and looking around. "It's late."

Zoran stood up as well. "I'll walk you back," he told her, taking her hand in his.

"That's not necessary," she told him, trying to pull back. The darkness was isolating now. It made their words seem much more intimate.

"I will not allow you to walk back to your cabin in this darkness."

She looked up at him. "How are you going to get back to your camp site?" she asked.

He faced her, pulling her closer. "Are you worried about me, Ciara?" he asked gently.

She swallowed, trying to figure out what was running through her mind. It was hard though, with his hands now on her waist. 'Yes," she finally admitted. "It's dark and there aren't a lot of paths that will get you back to where your tent is."

"I'll be fine," he assured her, thinking of the military training he'd gone through, most of which took place at night, trying to break through enemy lines. "I'm pretty stealthy. I won't disturb any of the bears while getting back to my tent." He didn't bother to tell her that his backpack, along with his tent and all of his gear, was only a few feet away. He hadn't really established a camp site, preferring to move around instead of coming back to the same place each night.

He walked beside her until they reached her cabin.

"This is it," she whispered, not wanting to wake up anyone else in the campground.

Zoran lifted his hand, pushing the wisps of hair back from her face. "I'm going to kiss you," he warned her.

Ciara smiled tremulously. "I would like that very much," she whispered back. She could feel her heart pounding in her chest and wondered if he could hear it. As he lowered his head, her whole body started trembling with fear and anticipation. And when his lips touched hers, gently at first, tentative, probing tenderly, she thought she might just go up in flames.

When her arms moved around his neck, Zoran deepened the kiss, wanting more, wanting to lift her up and carry her away so that he could make love to her properly. He wanted all of her. He wanted to possess her!

He settled for kissing her with everything inside of him, showing her the depths of his desire. When he pressed her back against the wall of her cabin, she moved against him, showing him that she was no longer afraid, that everything he was making her feel had overridden any fears that might have lingered after their long conversation.

She tilted her head, wanting the kiss to go on forever! When his lips were touching hers, she felt like she was flying, soaring high above the ground. She loved the roughness of his tongue as it invaded her mouth and she arched against his body, wanting so much more!

He slowly lifted his head as he gently pulled away and she was relieved that his breathing sounded as harsh as hers.

He could see the desire in her eyes but knew that it was too soon to act on that feeling. He'd have to pull back even though everything inside of him wanted to feel her wrapped around his body. She was so soft and beautiful. "Tomorrow. Meet me back at the tree line," he commanded.

His hand lifted up, touching her skin and she pressed her cheek against his palm. "Yes," she whispered.

A moment later, he was walking away and she felt cold and lonely. She waited until he was at the tree line again but then he stopped and turned around, watching her. She trembled, wanting to call him back or, even better, to run towards him and start that kiss all over again.

Instead, she walked into her cabin and hurried to the window. She almost laughed out loud when she saw his hand lift in farewell. How he knew that she was standing at her window, she'd never know. But she liked that he could read her so well.

Chapter 2

Ciara was on swimming duty today! She wouldn't be in the woods!

And she hadn't seen him on her run this morning. Where was he? Was he okay?

She pulled on her boring, one piece bathing suit after breakfast, grabbed a towel and pulled on a pair of shorts, not bothering with a tee-shirt today. She'd be in the water all day, but she couldn't argue with the camp director even though she had been hoping to be assigned a task that would put her more into the tree line. Unfortunately, her swimming assignment meant she wouldn't see Zoran!

But she'd see him tonight! That was something even though it was hours away.

She'd barely slept last night, thinking about that kiss, about how he made her feel just by looking at her.

As she picked her way over to the dock and started setting up the swimming games for the day, she thought about her future, something she tried to avoid thinking about whenever possible. She would be married soon – possibly earlier than planned because of the rising tensions with the countries bordering hers. Her father might love her, but he was a ruler above all else and if he could form a valuable alliance that could help protect the people in his country by marrying off his daughter, he would do it without remorse. It wasn't only because Ciara was a female. If she'd been born a male, the same would be true. Royal marriages were about alliances and forming a strong union that could help in an emergency. They weren't about love or spending the next fifty years with another person. Her marriage would be political and she'd accepted that a long time ago.

She should be a virgin on her wedding night, but the thought of another man touching her, someone other than Zoran, made her skin crawl. How had he gotten to her in such a short period of time? She barely knew the man!

About midday, she felt a strange sensation and looked around. She wasn't sure what it was, but she somehow knew that Zoran was watching her. Feeling self-conscious, she grabbed her towel and covered up. The kids were all heading into the showers to change anyway so no one would think it odd that she was drying off as well.

She picked up her backpack and checked her messages on her cell phone. Several from her father, a few from her friends...

Ciara almost dropped her phone when she saw the text message. "Drop the towel."

She looked around and just knew. He was watching her!

She bit her lip, wondering if she had the courage.

"Drop it now," came the next text and she shivered at the power that came through from his words.

She smiled, thinking about dropping the towel. It would be crazy, wouldn't it? Obviously he was watching her.

"You going to lunch, Ciara?" Joe called out. He and the lifeguard, Rosa, waited a moment.

Ciara shook her head. "Could you grab me a sandwich? I'm just going to get the ropes course ready for the next group."

Both Rosa and Joe nodded their heads. "Sure thing. We'll hurry back to help."

"No rush," she called back, thinking that Zoran was close by. She wanted to see him, just to let her eyes roam over him. That would be enough to sustain her until tonight.

The other two camp counselors walked off, chatting with each other as they made their way to the dining hall. When they were far enough away, she turned back, her eyes scanning the edge of the woods, trying to catch just a glimpse.

And then she saw him! He was swimming across the lake! Goodness, his hard body was crossing through the water as if it were nothing! She'd never seen anyone swim so well before; he was amazing.

When he stood up on the dock, she looked around, shocked to see him in shorts, dripping water.

"What are you doing here?" she demanded, worried that the camp director would see him. How could anyone miss him? He was huge! And glorious! And amazing!

"You didn't drop the towel, Ciara," he told her, his dark eyes glaring at her as he moved closer.

She smiled slightly, her body tingling with awareness of this man and how easily he could make her body sing with need. "I have to set up for the next class," she whispered, standing her ground but her whole body was trembling.

"Drop the towel." He kept coming closer.

She let it fall to the wooden deck, let his eyes move over her swimsuit clad body. When his eyes skimmed over her breasts, she felt her nipples pucker and knew that he could see everything.

His eyes snapped up to hers and she inhaled as she felt the heat from his gaze. "Tell me what has to happen before the kids return from lunch."

She told him and he smoothly dove back into the water. With both of them working together, all the ropes were connected properly and it took barely a fraction of the time it would normally take. When she told him it was finished, she felt his arms wrap around her and he pulled her over to the section of the water that was hidden from view from the campsite. As soon as they were out of view, his mouth covered hers and his hands slid up and down her body. Without the hindrance of regular clothing to stop him, it was practically as if she was naked.

He lifted her legs, showing her how to wrap them around his waist so that she could hold onto him and she clung to him while he kissed her. His hands moved to her breasts, sliding against the material and making her nipples even harder, more sensitive. She'd never in her life imagined such feelings and she shifted against him, wanting more.

"Shhh," he coaxed. "You don't want someone coming over here to find out what's going on."

Ciara bit her lip as his fingers slid the strap of her bathing suit down. "They'll be coming back soon," she whispered.

His eyes looked into hers as he slowly peeled her bathing suit down. The water was covering her but he lifted her higher, his eyes feasting on her breasts. When his mouth covered one taut peak, she couldn't hold back the cry of delight as her fingers dove into his hair, pulling and twisting as desire coiled inside of her.

When he lowered her back down, she could feel the tension in his own body. "We have to stop."

"No," she begged, leaning her forehead against his broad shoulder. "This is crazy," she sighed.

His hands were firm and confident as he held her against him, sliding up and down her back, moving to tease her breasts as well. "Meet me tonight. What time?"

Her arms were shaking and she wanted so badly to shift so that his hands would touch her nipples again, to feel that crazy sensation. But he was teasing her by not going there, by resisting those sensitized nubs. "I get off right after dinner again."

"Fine. Meet me at the edge of the tree line," he told her and pulled her straps back up. He kissed her one more time, then swam with her as they returned to the dock. "Until tonight," he told her and kissed her, hard and quick.

Ciara heard the excited voices of the campers as they approached the dock. Lunch was over. So was her time with Zoran. "You have to go," she urged him, not wanting to be caught with him in the lake.

"Next time, follow my orders," he said and ducked down under the water just as the first of the kids stepped onto the dock.

Ciara held her breath as he ducked under the water, not sure where he was going or how he was going to get out of sight. But she watched the smooth surface of the lake until she saw his head pop up again in the distance. If she hadn't known it was him, she wouldn't have noticed him. And none of the campers saw anything out of the ordinary. She was grateful for his discretion, but she still wished she'd had more time with him.

And she couldn't get out of the water!

Since her body still showed evidence of her desire for him, she swam out to one of the ropes course stations, waving to Joe and Rosa to indicate where she was.

The rest of the afternoon moved painfully slowly. She stayed in the water until the other campers rotated through. When the afternoon's activities were finally over, she pulled herself up on the dock, relieved that it was finally safe and her body wouldn't show any indications of her excitement after being with Zoran.

She didn't pick up her phone, afraid to see if there were other orders from Zoran. But she didn't pick up her towel as she helped the kids grab their belongings.

By dinner time, she was shaking. She'd showered and changed, but she hadn't dared to look at her phone, too afraid of what he might tell her to do. It wasn't that she didn't want to do it, she just was frightened of the intensity of what he made her feel. It was crazy and out of control.

She grabbed an apple for dinner, then made her way out of the dining hall. She wasn't on duty tonight so she took advantage of her "night off". Grabbing a book, she walked out to the tree line, thinking she'd just sit and read until Zoran showed up.

But he was already there!

"I wasn't supposed to be here for another hour," she told him, standing there looking at him. The sun was still shining down, but it was a soft, golden glow now.

"You ignored my messages."

He tried to hide his need for this slender beauty, but it was hard. He was hard. His mind was so focused on her that it was difficult to think of anything else.

"Yes," she told him, the book forgotten in her hands.

"Why?"

"Because..." she looked into his eyes, glad that she could see them tonight. Not for long, though, she realized. The sun was sinking over the horizon quickly. She had maybe an hour of sunlight left. "Because what you make me feel scares me. I don't understand it."

Zoran heard her words and relaxed slightly. It was exactly what he wanted to hear. Not that she was afraid of him. He didn't like that at all. "Trust me," he coaxed and took her hand, pulling her deeper into the tree line. "I won't hurt you."

She shook her head. "I think we will both hurt each other when we head back to real life."

"What's real?" he asked, thinking she might be right, but he didn't want to dwell on that. This woman, this moment, was his reality now. He didn't want to think about his responsibilities or the burden of ruling Larcatia right now. He wanted to focus everything he had on her. On her soft skin and listening to her voice. "Tell me about the swimming course today. It looked like fun."

She smiled, relieved that he wasn't going to pounce on her immediately. Oh, he'd better make a move by the end of the night, but at least she could relax slightly now. She told him what the kids had to do through each of the stations and he gave her ideas on other challenges for the kids. He didn't tell her that he'd gone through SEAL training with some of the US soldiers, or that some of the ideas he offered were from that tough course. They only had a limited amount of time with each other and he didn't want to dwell on issues that might raise too many questions. Questions he couldn't answer.

As the sun set and darkness surrounded them, he pulled her closer, having her lean against his chest while they talked. He didn't touch her in any other way, just enjoyed listening to her voice and her musical laughter.

Eventually, the tension around them grew thicker and their conversation died out, replaced by an intense awareness of each other. His hands moved along the skin of her arms and she froze, her breath catching in her throat.

When his fingers moved against her waist, she held her breath, praying that he would move them higher, to feel the crazy feelings that he'd given her earlier today.

"Tell me what you want me to do," he said in her ear.

"Touch me," she finally said.

"Where?" he asked, even though he knew. He just wanted to hear her say it.

Ciara bit her lip, unaware of how her hands where gripping his knees as she waited tensely for his hands to cup her breasts.

"Tell me where, Ciara," he urged, his teeth biting the shell of her ear.

She shook her head, unable to say the words, but she lifted his hands, showing him instead of telling him. When his fingers cupped her breast, she closed her eyes and leaned her head back against his shoulder. Those amazing fingers found her nipple through both layers of clothing and she arched into his hand.

She gasped when his hands moved away and her eyes sprung open, a sound of disapproval came out of her mouth but he shushed her again. A moment later, she stiffened in his arms when his large hands slid underneath her shirt. She couldn't believe how perfect those fingers felt. And then he pulled that shirt off over her head, wanting it gone.

"I want to see you," he told her.

Ciara had no idea what he could see, but she didn't care. She was too caught up in the moment, wanting his fingers back against her breasts. Her hands were impatient, grabbing them back and putting them on her breasts once again. With a flick of his fingers, he found and released the front clasp of her bra, then slowly pulled the lace back away.

She was holding her breath and she suspected that he was as well. Never before had she felt so powerful and so feminine.

"You're beautiful," he whispered as his fingers slid across her nipples. She gasped, the tender, almost-not-there touch sending her desire spiraling.

"Please!" she gasped.

A moment later, he shifted their positions. His tee-shirt was pulled off of his back and laid out underneath her as he held himself above her, looking down at her pale breasts in the moonlight. "Do you trust me?" he asked in a soft, rough sounding voice.

She nodded her head. "Yes," she told him to emphasize her response.

A moment later, his hand slid the zipper of her shorts down. She gasped and grabbed his wrist, stopping him, but he looked into her eyes. "Trust me," he coached softly.

He felt her fingers relax and slid the zipper down further. The lace of her underwear enticed him, but he didn't pull it down. He wanted to take this slowly but he was in so much pain.

Lowering his head, he captured her nipple in his mouth while smoothing his fingers down lower. Very gently, he slid his fingers into her heat, moving slowly so he wouldn't startle her. All the while, his mouth teased her nipples, biting, soothing, sucking and driving her wild. He loved the way she clenched his fingers, her body unable to hold still under his tender ministrations. The whole time, he wished that there was more light so that he could see her instead of just feel her.

Too soon, he felt her start to splinter apart and he absorbed her cry in his mouth as his fingers pulled her over her peak.

When she floated back down to earth, she opened her eyes and looked up at him, startled by what she'd just experienced. "That was…"

"Amazing," he finished when she couldn't come up with a description.

"Yes," she breathed, lifting her arms to circle around his neck. "Now what happens?"

He kissed her neck and her ear again before pulling away. "Now, you go back to your cabin and go to sleep." He zipped up her shorts again, his fingers deft and sure.

He lifted himself off of her, then bent down to pick her up as well.

Ciara was so stunned by that statement that she wasn't sure what to say. She didn't want to stop but she was suddenly shy and wrapped her arms around her naked breasts self-consciously. "I don't want to go back. And you…"

"I'm fine," he assured her.

She pressed her hands against his bare chest, feeling the tension within him. "You're not okay. I want to finish this," she told him, kissing the middle of his chest.

Zoran closed his eyes and wrapped his arms around her waist, pulling her closer. "We can't."

"Why not?" she demanded.

He kissed the top of her head. "Because you are a virgin."

She stiffened in his arms, not sure why his words hurt so much. "And?"

He pushed her away from him and shook his head. "And you need to walk away from me, Ciara. I'm not the man for you."

Ciara suddenly realized that she was standing in front of him, nearly naked and felt vulnerable. She quickly closed her bra, shifted her shorts and grabbed her shirt from the ground, knocking off the dirt before pulling it over her head.

Dressing gave her enough time to pull herself together and realize what she wanted. Him! "We're going to finish this tomorrow night, Zoran," she told him firmly. "Meet me here."

Zoran heard the words and would have liked nothing better. But this was not to be. She had to give her virginity to her husband. "I won't be here, Ciara." That husband couldn't be him. He had a political marriage waiting for him and he couldn't ignore his responsibilities.

She stiffened with his words and looked up at him. She could see the need in his eyes and her heart broke for this man because, instinctively, she knew that he was in pain and was stopping only because of his innate sense of honor.

She stepped closer, ignoring him when he stepped back. She reached out and touched the middle of his chest again. "Yes you will. And so will I. It's going to be wonderful."

With that, she walked away, running back to her cabin. Before she turned the corner, she looked back and saw him. Raising her hand, she nodded her head, silently telling him again that they would finish together tomorrow night.

Chapter 3

Ciara worried all the next day. She was in charge of the archery station and this was an area in which she excelled. Shooting and using a bow and arrow were a requirement of her education, so she was able to give solid advice to each of the campers as they came through her station. Even the guys in charge of the BB gun station came over to her when the weapons jammed. She was quickly able to fix them and even moved over to that area when one of the campers was really struggling, becoming discouraged by his lack of ability to hit the paper target.

But the whole day, she was wondering if Zoran would meet her that night. She had everything ready for him and she wasn't going to take no for an answer. The week was coming to an end and she would be heading home. She wasn't leaving here without experiencing the bliss of being in Zoran's arms, of fully becoming his woman.

What if he didn't show up? What if he decided that he couldn't follow through?

She would track him down, she told herself. Somehow, some way, she would get her security team to find him, to discover everything about him so that she could go to him. She had absolutely no idea how their future together could work, but somehow, she'd make it.

That night, she stood on the edge of the tree line, trembling because he wasn't there. "Zoran!" she called out a second time, her eyes filling with tears when she realized that he really wasn't there.

She slumped down onto a log, the same log they'd sat upon the first night when they'd talked for hours. She hadn't realized how uncomfortable it was without Zoran with her to distract her from the strange, unfamiliar night sounds.

After thirty minutes, she accepted that he really wasn't going to show up. She couldn't stop the tears that started flowing or the pain of loss in her heart. She wanted him so desperately and he'd simply abandoned her! How could he?!

Zoran watched from the shadows as she sat there, her eyes scanning the darkness for any sign of him. But she wouldn't see him. He'd watched her all day long, was proud of her skill with the bow and arrow, impressed with her rifle skills even though it was just a small, kids' toy. But she was accurate and patient with the other kids.

He couldn't go out there. For the first time in his life, he was trying to be noble with a woman because there could be no future with Ciara. The other woman in his past knew the rules, understood the temporary nature of any liaison with him. Ciara was different. He felt differently towards her. He would return home at the end of this week and would marry the bride his father was choosing for him. He had no idea who it was, nor did he care. He would do his duty and marry whichever woman, but he would always treasure these moments with Ciara.

His resolve lasted only until he saw the tears on her cheeks. Women had tried tears on him many times in the past, several of them calling him a cold-hearted bastard for the way he remained unmoved, irritated even, by their overflowing emotions.

Some of those tears had probably been genuine and others just a futile attempt to manipulate him. But Ciara's tears tore at him, stabbed him with each drop that fell to her soft cheeks.

When he accepted that he couldn't take it any longer, he stepped into the area, lifting her into his arms. "Don't cry, love," he told her, his voice rough as he sat back down with her on his lap.

"You're here!" she sobbed, wrapping her arms around his neck. "I didn't think you'd show up. But you're here!"

"I'm here," he told her, kissing her tenderly, and when he felt her lips tremble under his and then respond to his kiss, he deepened the caress, forcing her lips open so that his tongue could move inside, soothe her in the only way he knew how.

"Stop!" she said when his hands moved underneath her tee-shirt.

"What's wrong?" he asked but his hands stilled.

Ciara shook her head and stood up. "Come with me," she told him. She was nervous but also determined. This was her man. Zoran was hers and she intended to show him tonight.

Zoran wasn't sure what she was going to do but he took her hand and followed her. It was only when they were almost at her cabin that he stopped, pulling her to a stop.

"No, Zoran. You're coming with me," she told him firmly, her fingers pulling at his arm futilely. The man was big and strong and stubborn. If he didn't want to go somewhere, he wasn't going.

"This isn't right, Ciara. You should…"

She moved in closer, pressing her body against his in an effort to convey her message more clearly. "No. Stop talking. I'm in charge tonight," she told him. "You had your way with me last night. Tonight, it is my turn."

He chuckled that such a little thing was going to try and overpower him. "Think so?" he teased.

She pulled back when his hands reached out for her. "I know so. Now march," she ordered, tangling her fingers with his.

Zoran laughed softly, aware that others might be close by. He didn't want her to get into trouble, but he was fascinated by this woman and her attempt at taking control.

"We're not making love tonight, Ciara," he told her.

Ciara stood on the first step of her tiny cabin and she was still shorter than he was. "Zoran, if you don't get inside that doorway, I'm going to strip down right here and we'll both discover what is going to happen."

He chuckled and crossed his arms over his massive chest. "You're not going to strip down here, Ciara. Too much potential for someone to see you."

She raised one eyebrow in challenge, both irritated by his stubbornness and turned on by the feminine power she felt surging through her. She knew that he wanted her. Badly. And she was going to follow through on all of her desires tonight. "Really?" she asked with a secret smile.

A moment later, he cursed under his breath when she simply lifted her tee-shirt over her head. Zoran lifted her from the step and carried her the rest of the way into the cabin. "That's cheating, Ciara," he told her.

She didn't listen. She stepped back and reached behind her. Zoran noticed her shaking hands, but his mind was focused only on her breasts. They looked perfect in the moonlight, pale and pert, full with beautiful, pink nipples that were begging him for his mouth. She dropped the bit of lace onto the floor and Zoran watched in fascination as her fingers moved to the waistband of her shorts. A moment later, she did a little twist thing and the shorts fell to the floor. She stood there in only her lace underwear and he thought he'd just died and gone to heaven.

"Stop," he told her but the command wasn't as firm as it normally was and, as expected, she ignored it.

Her fingers moved to the elastic and he groaned. Dropping to his knee, he pushed her hands out of the way while his own fingers took control. He pulled the elastic away from her soft skin, enjoying the feeling of it against the backs of his hands. But every part of him was focused on her, on the sweet smell of Ciara.

When his hands reached out to pull her into his arms, she quickly stepped backwards.

She was trembling but she wasn't going to let him have his way tonight. This was her night and she had plans. Big plans for this enormous, gentle giant. "No, Zoran. You only get to look until you're equally divested of obstacles," she told him with that sweet smile that told him she'd planned this out carefully.

71

Zoran straightened up, towering over her. "And if I don't?" he asked, his eyes boring into hers.

She shrugged her shoulders. "Then you don't get to touch me tonight." She bit her lip and considered her next words carefully. "I'll do it all myself." She could not believe that she'd actually said that. But it worked like magic. There was a stunned moment of silence as he absorbed her words but then he chuckled slightly. His hands reached out and pulled his black tee-shirt off, dumping it over her bra and underwear. He stepped closer, intending to take her into his arms but she shook her head. "No. I've seen it all from a distance. I want to see it up close and personal now."

He smiled down at her. "You think you're taking control, don't you?" he asked, but it wasn't really a question. It was a promise. "Ah, little one, you have so much to learn." But he was helpless against her appeal. He wanted her. His body ached to possess her. And she was too beautiful to resist.

"Then you'd better start teaching me," she whispered back to him, looking up into his eyes. She let her hand move slowly down his chest, fascinated by all of the rippling muscles she discovered. But when her fingers touched the waistband of his cargo pants, he grabbed her hands, not letting her go any further.

"My turn," he told her. He stepped backwards, his eyes holding her captive just like that first time. And with slow hands, he released the button on his pants, then the zipper. A moment later, he shoved both his pants and his boxers down, stepping out of his clothes, his boots and socks already gone.

Then he stood up in full, glorious nakedness, in front of her.

Ciara could barely breathe as she looked her fill, amazed and more than a little astonished by how large he was. That erection didn't look as big and intimidating from a distance. But she wanted this, she told herself. Every part of her was aching to discover what it was like to be a part of this man, to have him fill her up.

With shaking hands, she reached out and touched him. Her fingers were too soft at first but he wrapped his fingers around her hand, showing her how he liked to be touched, stroked. When she bent down, he shook his head with a pained chuckle. "No way, Ciara."

"But..." she started to argue.

"Another time. I'm too close already." And with that, he lifted her effortlessly into his arms and carried her the few additional feet to her tiny bed. Laying her down, he stood up and looked at her.

She started to sit up. "I'm in charge tonight," she told him and jumped up, only slightly self-conscious about being naked in front of him. Yes, she wanted to cover herself up. But the way his eyes were watching her gave her a sense of power.

She put her hands on his shoulders, pressing him back to the bed. "You sit down."

Even in the darkness, Zoran could see her blushes. Or maybe he could just feel them. He thought it was adorable that she thought she could take control but he allowed it for a few more minutes, wondering what she was going to do next.

"Okay, I'm on the bed. Now what?" he teased.

Ciara stood there in front of him, not really sure what to do. She was trembling now, her whole body aching with anticipation but…what should she do?

"Come here, Ciara," Zoran commanded, seeing her distress and not liking it one little bit.

She moved the few inches closer, wishing she'd thought this out more thoroughly. Or at least listened to her friends as they'd described their sexual escapades. She'd heard several of the other camp counselors had hooked up over the summer. Why hadn't she taken notes?

Because until she'd met this man, sex had never really interested her. It had been something far off in the distance, something that she couldn't have so she wouldn't let herself think about it.

Unfortunately for her aching body, she'd been thinking of almost nothing else for the past three days. And still she was stumped.

Zoran watched her features and would have laughed if he weren't in so much pain. Instead of waiting for her to figure out what the next move might be, he took her hand and pulled her forward until she was sitting on his lap. "As much as I appreciate the effort, you're going to listen to me tonight. Okay?"

She sighed with relief and delight, wrapping her arms around his neck. "Okay," she replied happily.

He bent his head and kissed her, feeling her trembling increase but now it was with excitement instead of trepidation. With one arm on her back, his other smoothed down her sides, tempting her back to passion. It didn't take long before the need and urgency overrode her inhibitions.

With his fingers and his mouth, he explored Ciara, finding all of the parts of her that pushed her desire higher. And when his mouth covered that secret part of her, she exploded apart and Zoran knew that this time, it was better than the previous night.

And then it hit him. He didn't have any protection!

"Ciara, we can't…"

Her small fists gripped his shoulders. "Don't say that!" she gasped as she slowly came back to reality after that explosive climax. "You promised me."

He shook his head. "First of all, I didn't promise you anything. In fact, if it were up to me, you'd still be clothed, I'd be watching over your cabin again and you'd be fast asleep."

"And secondly?" she prompted, letting her hands move over his amazing chest.

"Secondly, I can't risk getting you pregnant. I wasn't anticipating this. I didn't bring any protection."

The smile that curled her beautiful lips at that moment startled him. When she reached into a drawer beside her bed, he almost groaned with gratitude. And then anger. "Where did you get this?" he asked, lifting the condom from her fingers.

She licked her lips as her eyes moved down over his arms and lower. "I asked one of the other camp counselors if she had any to spare."

The anger eased over the news that she hadn't had these handy because of previous lovers. "Why do I get the impression that there is more to this story?"

She let her fingers roam down low on his stomach, almost laughing at the way his stomach muscles clenched. "She gave me a whole box," Ciara whispered.

Zoran almost laughed. If he hadn't been so hard, so ready to fill her up, he might have. But the idea that this woman had obtained more than one condom, was expecting an entire night of sexual exploration…with him…made him lose his focus. Again!

"You're not going to be able to walk tomorrow," he growled as he tore open the package and rolled the latex down his erection.

Positioning himself between her legs, he pulled her closer. "Are you sure about this Ciara?" he cautioned.

She smiled up at him. "Very sure," she told him, lifting her knees so that her legs were cradling him. "So sure, and so excited, you can't even know."

He pushed himself into her, his eyes closing as he felt her tight sheath. Inch by inch, he moved into her heat and pulled out. When he was pressing deeper, he opened his eyes and looked down at her. She was stiff and nervous and this definitely wasn't going to work, he thought. He'd never been with a virgin before, but he had enough experience with women to know that he didn't want Ciara to be looking like she was being tortured.

"Look at me, Ciara," he told her and he didn't move until she opened her eyes. "What's wrong?" he demanded.

Ciara couldn't believe he was asking her this right at this particular moment. "Zoran, I'm sure that there is a time for talking, but is this really it?"

He nodded his head. "Absolutely. You look like you're about to face an executioner. Am I hurting you?"

He moved a bit more, not pressing any deeper and he felt her muscles clench around him, tightening her silken grip.

Leaning on one arm, he shifted his angle, letting one hand move against her again.

"You're just a bit bigger than I was anticipating."

He chuckled. "And you're such a little thing," he said, his hand moving to cup her breast. His thumb moved and tweaked her nipple. "I think I like you in this position. You can't boss me around."

"Not that it ever worked," she gasped out. His thumb and forefinger worked that nipple and she felt it right down to her core. Her hips shifted involuntarily, taking more of him, pulling him in deeper. She grabbed his hand, needing to focus on the other parts of him. "Zoran, this isn't…"

"Stop talking," he told her.

She laughed. "You just ordered me to talk to you," she replied.

"Now I want you to feel," he said and bent lower, his teeth nibbling against her throat. "I want you to do that again," he said and his fingers did the same thing to her nipple. Sure enough, she gasped and arched again, taking him even deeper. He helped her by pulling out and moving into her again, slowly, taking her body's movements into play. His fingers moved down her back, her side, teasing all of the sensitive spots he'd discovered before. But this time, each time she shifted against him, he pushed deeper before pulling out. It took only a few minutes of this teasing before she was gasping once again, begging him to fill her, to finish this. He wouldn't.

Sweat beaded his forehead and back as he struggled to go slowly. It wasn't until she once again wrapped her legs around his hips and she pulled him deeper that he felt the barrier of her virginity. And in a split second, it broke and he was able to bury himself right to the hilt, filling her up and she felt better than any woman ever had.

"Don't stop!" she begged, almost punching his shoulder.

Zoran would have chuckled at her persistence in trying to take charge but he decided that her orders and his desires were in complete accord. He moved in and out of her again, listening to her gasps of pleasure. Over and over again, he took her higher, closer to that peak.

"Let yourself go, Ciara," he coaxed, and his hand moved lower, finding that bud that would spin her out of control. As soon as he touched her, she splintered apart, her body arching up to his and he took her scream into his mouth, kissing her hard while he pumped into her until he found his own release. He held her close on the ridiculously small bed while the waves of pleasure floated them both back down to earth. When they were finished, he switched their positions so that he was on the bed and she was laying on top of him. It was the only way that they could both fit on the bed and even then, his feet were hanging off the end by about another foot.

"Oh my," she sighed as she rested her cheek against his chest, listening to his heart beat slow down.

His hands were sifting through her hair, letting it fall against his overly sensitive skin. "I agree," he growled.

She lifted her head, resting her chin on her stacked hands. "Would you really have walked away from me?" she asked softly.

He paused for a moment. "Yes," he finally admitted. He looked into her eyes while his mind tried to figure out what was going on inside of him. She confused him, rattled him and did things to him that he didn't fully understand. He wasn't sure if he liked it either.

One thing he was sure of, he wasn't letting this woman get away from him. He would keep her somehow, even if she had to be his mistress, he would figure out a way.

Chapter 4

Ciara woke up the following morning alone but she smiled as she stretched sore muscles. Over and over again, Zoran had woken her up to make love to her throughout the night. She should be exhausted, but instead, she was energized. She felt like a new woman! It was amazing what a great night of almost unending sex could do to a woman!

And she loved him! Goodness, how she loved him! He was so tender at times and then demanding and powerful. She loved both ways, feeling as if she were on top of the world when he touched her. When she climaxed in his arms, she knew that she could fly. It was one of the most amazing experiences and she couldn't wait until tonight.

She was hurrying to get to the dining hall so she could help set up for breakfast when she realized that nothing had been said about tonight. Or the future!

She stopped in her tracks, looking around. Could there even be a future with Zoran? Had her father already arranged for her marriage? It was possible and her body chilled at the idea. Surely he wouldn't negotiate for her marriage without consulting her, would he?

Of course he would. He had to! It was both his right and his responsibility. And until this week, she'd accepted that. But now, knowing Zoran and his lovemaking, she couldn't go through with it! She couldn't accept another man into her body!

If she hadn't met him, if she hadn't known the beauty of his touch, she might have gone blindly into her wedding and never known what real love could be like. But now she did know! And she couldn't settle!

Oh goodness, this was not going to be a happy reunion with her father!

And she was fairly certain that Zoran would never be satisfied with being her secret lover.

She had no idea what she was going to do!

"You okay, Ciara?" the camp director asked.

Ciara realized that she was just standing in the middle of the camp, almost hyperventilating.

77

She closed her eyes and forced herself to calm down. "Yes. I'm fine, but thanks." Except that she wasn't fine! She was miserable and she couldn't believe that she was in this situation! It was untenable!

"You okay?" the text came through. There was no name attached to it, but she knew that Zoran was watching her. How had he gotten her phone number? Ciara smiled, thinking that the man definitely had a way of finding things out.

She looked up at the mountains and across the lake, trying to figure out where he was. But he wasn't anywhere to be seen. Her secret lover, she thought with a smile.

"I'm fine," she texted right back. "You're coming back to me tonight, right?" she asked.

There was silence and she stared at her cell phone, willing him to respond.

"Don't do this to me," she texted back. "Please don't throw this away. I'm only here until the end of this week. Let's share our nights until then."

Still silence.

"Please," she texted again.

She wasn't proud that she was begging, but she'd do anything to see him again. They might have known each other for only a couple of days but she knew that she loved him with every part of her and she wanted him for as long as possible. If that was only a few days, then she wanted to have those days.

Ciara almost threw her phone into the lake when the silence continued. Instead, she stomped into the dining hall and focused on her responsibilities. She made the drinks, set up the plates, prepared the tables and made sure that things were ready. When the first set of kids and counselors started arriving, she made herself so busy sweeping and mopping, hurrying around to help out in any way possible, all so that she wouldn't have to think about Zoran not coming to her tonight.

The whole day, she worked hard, checking her text messages over and over again until she finally just shut it off. He wasn't coming, she told herself. He was staying away out of some stupid sense of honor, trying to protect her innocence. Well, she was the one who should be able to decide on what she wanted and didn't want. It was one thing if he didn't want her anymore. He should just be a man and tell her that to her face if that was the case. But for him to decide that they couldn't be together simply because he thought she might get hurt at the end of their affair, well, he was just being stupid! And it was pure rubbish!

By the time the bonfire was lighting up the sky, she was so angry with his continued silence that she stayed with the campers. They told ghost stories and camp stories, laughed at some of the skits. The kids all went off to their bunks and she stayed behind, cleaning up the area, making sure that the fire was completely out, then she went to the dining hall, hanging out with the other counselors who were relaxing. There were only three more days until the end of the summer. The camp would close down for the season and all of these people would head back to their colleges or jobs. Many of them were teachers during the school year and spent their summers at the camp to earn extra money. Others were college students. She was fairly certain that she was the only princess in the group. And she'd had to beg her father to let her work here. If it weren't for the rising tensions and the kidnapping threat, he probably never would have allowed her to work outside the palace.

In the end, he'd been convinced that she was more protected here – where no one would think to look for her – than she was if she were to leave the palace for any reason.

As Ciara walked slowly back to her tiny cabin that night, she felt like her whole world had darkened. Zoran was gone, trying to be an honorable man. And she was alone.

She curled up on her cot, not even changing into pajamas. She didn't want to sleep, she thought. She wanted to scream out in pleasure with Zoran's arms around her, to feel his muscles clench as he climaxed in her arms and then fall on top of her, his weight on her smaller body like a reward.

She must have dozed because something startled her awake. She had no idea what it was, but she sat up in bed.

And there he was! His hands were fisted by his sides and he looked furious as he watched her.

"Zoran!" she gushed, so relieved to see him. But the look he was giving her held her back. "What's wrong?"

He looked down at the slender woman laying on top of the blankets. He was furious with himself for his lack of discipline, his inability to stay away from Ciara. "I shouldn't be here."

She stood up, angry now. "Says you! You were going to vanish without any word, without telling me goodbye!"

"Yes," he replied, confirming her accusation. "It is for the best."

"Whose best?" she came back furiously but trying to keep her voice down so that she didn't wake up the staffers in the nearby cabins. "Yours? Because it certainly isn't better for me! And don't you dare claim to be able to tell me what's right and wrong for me! I won't let you be that arrogant!"

She was so angry with him that she punched him. It wasn't hard, but it showed him how furious she was that he would take the decision making into his own hands. "If you don't want me, then just say it! If one night was enough, fine! But be a man and tell me that to my face!"

He grabbed her wrists, holding her against him. "It wasn't enough. And you are better off without me here. It is wrong. There's no future for us."

She wanted to kick him but instead, she pressed her body against his. "Who says I want a future?" she whispered. "I just want you for as long as I can have you."

He hesitated for another long moment. He fought the battle inside of him and lost. He needed her. He'd tried to stay away, but she was like a siren, pulling him closer. He'd seen the way she'd worked herself ragged around the camp today and he didn't like it. So here he was, unable to stay clear and wanting nothing more than to wrap his arms around her and make love to her until she was too exhausted to argue with him any longer.

"We'll probably regret this," he growled but he pulled her to him. Pressing her down, he didn't even bother with the bed this time. It was too small and uncomfortable. He took her to the floor, pulling her blankets down to cushion their lovemaking.

Ciara thrilled to his touch. Tonight was different from the previous night. He was insatiable and, with the possibility of not seeing him again, so was she. Every time she started to drift off to sleep, she rolled over and started making love to him again.

By the time the breakfast bell woke her the following morning, she was alone, exhausted and sore. But she was also smiling as she hurried down the pathway to the dining hall.

Chapter 5

The next few nights were the best of Ciara's life. And the worst. Every moment that she spent in his company, she felt renewed. He took her higher than she'd ever thought possible and showed her things about her body that she never could have known. And she laughed. Goodness, how she laughed. He was a horrible tease, loved to tickle her once he'd discovered all of the places on her body that were so sensitive. And he was the most passionate, demanding lover! He wouldn't let her go halfway. And she loved every moment of her time in his arms.

But much too quickly, Friday arrived. She'd known this time was coming but she had wanted to stick her head in the sand and pretend that it was far away.

The night was giving way to the day and she couldn't hold back the tears any longer. "I have to go home tonight," she told him, laying on top of him with her cheek against his chest. It was her favorite position because it was the best way to feel as much of him against her skin as she could.

"Where do you live?" he asked, running his fingers through her hair. He was leaving tonight too. It was the end of his annual vacation and his father was already calling him back. He'd ignored two summons already but he couldn't ignore any further requests.

With his question, he felt her tense up.

"You wouldn't believe me if I told you," she sighed.

Zoran thought about his own role and had to chuckle. "I'm pretty hard to surprise." He felt her smile against his chest.

"I live in Altair." She turned so she could see his face.

Zoran froze, his fingers halting in mid caress. "Altair? You're kidding." So much for being hard to surprise, he thought. He was stunned!

She shook her head. "Nope. Have you been there? It's beautiful. Some say it is a bit wild, but they only hear the rumors."

"I've been there. Many times. I'm from Larcatia."

Ciara lifted her head, her palms pressing against his chest so she could look into his eyes. It was only then that the hard jawline and the dark eyes struck a memory. She tilted her head as she tried to remember the one portrait she'd seen in the

Larcatia palace. "No! Please tell me that you're not Zoran del Hassar Alzar, Crown Prince of Larcatia," she whispered.

Zoran rolled so that she was underneath him once more. "Princess Ciara," he mumbled. "Where the hell have you been?" he almost laughed out loud, delighted with this discovery.

She laughed as well, her fingers diving into his dark hair once more. "I've been hiding out here at a remote summer camp."

"And being a very naughty girl," he said, taking her nipple in his mouth and sucking, causing her to gasp out loud and arch as the fire reignited.

"I've been corrupted by an arrogant prince," she countered and shifted against him, causing him to hiss as she'd intended. "I think that I'm going to have to punish you for all of the naughty things that you've done."

Zoran chuckled as he grabbed her hands and pulled them up above her head. "I think that you should be thanking me for bringing you into the real world, princess," he said as his head descended to her other breast. He could feel her holding her breath as he hovered right above the pink nipple. "You're going to have to marry me, you understand that don't you?"

She wiggled underneath him, trying desperately hard to get him to follow through on where his lips were hovering. "You've endeavored all week to try and get me to do what you want, but so far I've resisted. What makes you think that I'm going to bow down to your commands now?"

His knee pressed between her legs and she willingly opened them for his penetration. She understood his silent message, her body waiting, desperately need him to follow through with that action but he stopped, not giving her what she wanted. "You're cheating," she said breathlessly.

"Admit that we're going to get married and I'll give you anything you want."

"I agree," she gasped. A moment later she was rewarded for her agreement when he pressed into her, filling her up. From that moment on, there was no more talking. Only feeling.

Chapter 6

Zoran stepped down out of the helicopter and quickly made his way through the palace. He barely took notice of the guards who were standing sentry outside of his father's office before he burst through the doors.

His eyes took in his father sitting behind the elaborate desk, his eyes looking tired, slightly strained. He thought about delaying the conversation until he understood what had happened over the past seven days, but this subject was too important. Everything else needed to take a back seat to the issue of his marriage. "I'm marrying Princess Ciara from Altair," he told his father.

Sheik Patir's mouth fell open in stunned silence for a long moment. But as his son's words sank into his exhausted brain, he rallied quickly, shaking his head in denial. "The contracts for your marriage have already been signed," his father said with a sigh, shaking his head and leaning back in the large, leather chair that had held the sheiks of Larcatia for centuries.

Zoran shook his head. "No, an alliance with Altair would be beneficial to both of our countries. With all of the increasing tensions on the borders, we will need their support in order to gain the upper hand. In fact, after this marriage, there might not be any more tensions. There are several issues that potentially could go away with an alliance between Larcatia and Altair."

His father rubbed his forehead, revealing more of his fatigue. "Except that your marriage contracts have been agreed to between Princess Jalayla bin Faisal of Tularia. The negotiations were finalized last Wednesday and all the contracts signed, sealed and delivered to the appropriate authorities, myself included, as of Thursday. That was the main reason I kept trying to call you back." He looked at his son with both pride at the man he'd become and a tinge of sadness that Zoran had finally found a woman he could love and it could not be.

Zoran shook his head, refusing to give up a life with Ciara. "Call King Busar and tell him that plans have changed."

Zoran's father stood up, shocked that his son would even suggest such a thing.

He leaned against his desk, his fists holding him up as he glared furiously at Zoran. "You know that we can't do that," his father uttered with finality. "The repercussions of such a move might shift the tensions into total war. We cannot insult the people of Tularia with a rejection of their princess. It simply isn't done. You know this, I shouldn't have to tell you such a thing."

Zoran ran a hand over his face in frustration. "There has to be something that can be done."

His father's eyes narrowed as he looked at Zoran, realizing there was much more to this discussion than what he'd heard so far. "What have you done?"

Zoran's hands flexed as he put them onto his hips. He wasn't afraid of his father. They had a good relationship with each other but this was something that he wasn't backing down on. "I met Princess Ciara while I was away."

The shock vibrating from his father rose into the air between the two men. "Tell me you didn't do anything stupid," his father demanded.

Zoran laughed, his head shifting back and forth as he remembered everything he had shared over the past week with the beautiful woman. "I did nothing stupid." He looked at his father "I will tell you that I fell in love with her. And she's agreed to marry me."

There was another very pregnant moment. "Impossible!" his father roared.

Zoran squared off with his father. "Not only is it possible, but it is going to happen. I'm marrying Princess Ciara." He moved closer to his father's desk. "This isn't hard to fix," he said to his father. "This is actually a very good thing."

His father's face looked almost apoplectic. "You cannot break an agreement of this magnitude. You will marry Princess Jalayla." He moved around his desk, coming closer to his son. "You've never shirked your duties before like this. How can you come in here and tell me that you didn't do anything stupid, and yet you're telling me that you're going to ignore a contract that commits yourself to another ruler's daughter?"

Zoran crossed his arms over his massive chest as he looked at his father. They were approximately the same height and they also had similar personalities. In the past, that had been cause for a few clashes. Two arrogant, stubborn men arguing over things that they both believed to be right did not make for a peaceful coexistence. But over the years, they had learned to adjust to each other's personalities and work with each other. The trials and tribulations, not to mention the enormous burden of responsibility that rested on the shoulders of the ruler, had forged a bond between these two men that was stronger than most fathers and sons.

But this was something about which Zoran was not backing down. There was no way that he could let go of Ciara in order to marry another woman. It didn't matter about the consequences. He would deal with the consequences later. Contracts were broken all the time. They just needed to be dealt with in a diplomatic way.

Zoran thought through the issues quickly, his agile mind coming up with several different solutions. "Send Simon over to Altair and explain the situation. Tell him to discuss possible negotiations, and that we are sincerely sorry for any insult that might be perceived. You know that this kind of thing can be undone," he said to his father.

Patir shook his head. "It can be done under normal circumstances but you know what has been happening on the borders over the past few months. We don't even truly understand why it is happening. If we could understand the tensions, this might be something that we could pull out of. But because the tensions are so out of character for all of these villages, we have to act carefully. You have to marry Princess Jalayla."

"I love her," Zoran said with a tone that would brook no argument.

His father paused for a moment, his eyes revealing his surprise. But then he rallied, his mind coming back to the repercussions to his country. "You will love who I tell you to love," his father roared.

Zoran smiled, understanding his father's anger at the moment. He wasn't going to give in, but he could understand the burden he'd just placed on the man. His father was a reasonable man and Zoran accepted that he needed to approach this in a different manner.

"Let's talk about the benefits of a union with Altair versus a union with Tularia." He paced back and forth, his mind sifting through all of the details that he knew about each of the countries. For the next hour, he and his father discussed the matter in greater detail, hashing out the pros and cons of each alliance. Initially, the discussion was heated. But as Zoran worked through all of the benefits, his father started to understand that a connection with Altair would have more benefits, both economic and political, rather than an alliance with Tularia.

By the time they were sitting down to dinner, his father was eagerly discussing ways that the contract with Tularia could be broken.

Chapter 7

Ciara stepped out of the limousine carefully, remembering all of the lessons on deportment that she had eliminated from her mind during her summer of freedom as she was now viewing her summer camp employment. She had carefully observed the other camp counselors over the summer camp and had tried to mimic their body movements. The rest of the world was much more casual in the way they walked or held themselves. But now she was back in Altair and she needed to remember all of the ways in which she needed to hold herself. The press would be watching her, the world would be watching her. She had disappeared for three months with no word to anyone. Even the paparazzi were out in droves, tripping over each other in their attempts to catch a picture of her returning to the palace.

She laughed softly as she listened with half an ear to some of their questions. "How was your time in rehab?" one of them called out. "Are all of the bruises healed?" another one yelled. "What does the baby look like?" yet another reporter asked over the din of all of the other silly questions.

So, they thought she had either suffered a drug overdose, was battered by a lover or perhaps her father, or she had given birth to a secret child. Did any of them remember the fact that she had just run a marathon before she'd disappeared? It was pretty hard to run twenty-six point two miles when pregnant or on a drug high.

Instead of dignifying any of their off-the-wall questions, she simply walked through the gates of the palace with her head held high and a secret smile hiding the love and excitement that she was feeling.

Her first priority was to find her father and find out what had happened over the past three months. Hopefully they had figured out who had been sending all of those disgusting kidnapping threats. She couldn't even be angry about those any longer because, first of all, she had been allowed to participate in an activity that she never would have been able to do had she been able to maintain her responsibilities for the government over the past three months. But best of all, she never would have met Zoran. Her love for that man swelled within her, and she felt in her pocket for the diamond ring that he had slipped on her finger only moments before she'd stepped onto a plane.

How he had discovered her departure time, not to mention which airport she was flying out of was a mystery. But she didn't care. That diamond ring signified that he was serious about his question from early this morning. He wanted to marry her! And she'd said yes! As if there could be any other answer.

Goodness, what a shocking change that had occurred over the past seven days. She'd met a man, fallen in love, and become engaged all within the past seven days. Never would she have thought this was possible. Her life before last week had been so predictable, so dull and tedious. She'd accepted her role, knew that she was an important member of this government. But she'd never had any excitement in her life, not in the way that Zoran gave her excitement every time he looked at her or touched her.

Ciara almost tripped over nothing as she thought back to the nights in Zoran's arms. She shook her head and looked around, hoping none of the other palace staff had noticed her misstep. It would be hard to explain how she'd tripped just thinking about a man from another country.

She had to get her mind off of the way that she felt when Zoran was close to her. She had to be cautious about all of this in order to convince her father that it was a good thing that she was going to marry Zoran. Hopefully, he hadn't started negotiations for any other marriage for her. If he had, she would just have to convince him that this was a better alliance.

"Hello, Father," she said as she stepped into the salon where they normally had drinks before dinner. "Hello, Mother," she said and bent low to give her mother a kiss on her cheek.

Her mother looked up at her beautiful daughter, knowing that something had changed. "What's going on?" her mother asked immediately.

Ciara laughed softly as she accepted the drink that the servant handed to her. "Thank you so much for this," she said to the servant. "Would you mind stepping out of the room for just a moment?" She turned to her mother and father with excitement in her soft, brown eyes. "I have something that I need to discuss with both of you. And it needs to be deliberated in private."

The doors to the salon were immediately closed behind the servant who had been preparing the drinks. When they were finally alone, Ciara turned to her parents and looked at them with all of the love she felt for Zoran shining through in her eyes. "I met a man, and I fell in love with him."

There was a tense silence for a long moment as her mother and father stared at her. The silence stretched out, her parents looking towards each other, then back at Ciara as their mouths fell open. "Tell me you are joking," her mother said in a choked voice.

"You can't be serious," her father commanded sitting up from the relaxed pose he'd been in to one of stiff horror. As his daughter's words sunk in, his eyes narrowed and he placed his glass of scotch on the table beside him with an angry clank. "If this is true, then I want to know the name of the man. Immediately."

Ciara smiled gently at both of her parents. "You're not to believe this," she said and folded her hands on top of her knees. "It's actually a pretty funny story. Neither of us realized who the other person was. But over the course of a week, I got to know Prince Zoran of Larcatia. He just happened to be hiking and camping in the woods near the summer camp in which I was working. I discovered that he's a very fascinating man. We fell in love and he proposed to me." She slipped a hand into her pocket and came back with the beautiful diamond ring in her hand. Very slowly she slipped the ring onto her finger, staring at it with all of the love that she felt for the man glowing in her eyes.

Her mother looked down at the ring then back up at her daughter. "But you are already engaged," she said. "We were going to announce your engagement to Prince Tasir of Lurasa." She hesitated for a long moment, "The announcement has all been arranged, reviewed and is set to be released to the press!"

Ciara looked from her mother to her father, wondering if this was all some sort of strange joke. "Please tell me that you're not serious about this." She'd known that her father would most likely arrange for her marriage at some point, but why did it have to be right now? When she'd finally met the man who could make her body sing with happiness? Her eyes darted back to her mother, realizing that this wasn't a joke. This was serious.

"Has the announcement been released?" she asked hurriedly, every muscle in her body tensing with trepidation as she waited for the answer.

Her parents looked towards each other once more, then back to her. "No, we were going to get the two of you together before any announcement was released. But the contracts have been signed, the negotiations all finalized. Everything is in place except for the two of you getting together and deciding on the minor details of the announcement," her father explained.

Ciara looked at her parents and the tension that had been growing inside of her chest eased someone with this news. "Well then there doesn't seem to be an enormous problem." She breathed in a deep breath, her hand moving to her chest to try and calm her racing nerves. "We can just contact everyone and explain that the contract needs to be negated."

Her father's mouth opened and closed, his confusion and anger increasing at her casual words and dismissal of such an important subject. "We can't just negate a contract. It simply isn't done. We have been friends with this country for years, decades even! We can't just pretend like the contracts have not been signed. The insult to the people of Lurasa would be intense. I cannot imagine ever breaking a contract like this."

Ciara's hand floated up to her mouth as she considered all of the ramifications for what she was proposing. "But wouldn't an alliance with Larcatia make more sense?" She asked both of them, her hands floating up into the air. "I mean, don't they have those oilfields that are very close to our border that have been causing problems for the past ten years or so?"

Her mother and father looked at each other once again. Her father nodded slightly to her mother. "Well, yes, that has been a problem. But we were going to try and figure out a different way to deal with that."

Ciara remembered all of the benefits and, just as Zoran had done with his father, she started to list the advantages of an alliance with Larcatia. She wouldn't relent on her arguments until she started to see the tension ease in her parents' eyes. By the time dinner was served, her mother and father finally agreed with her. The next step was trying to figure out how to cancel the contract between the two countries without insulting Prince Tasir.

Chapter 8

Ciara paced back and forth across the marble floor in front of her father's office. She didn't even realize how she was twisting her hands together, rubbing the skin almost raw. This was her life, this was all of her hopes and dreams that had been suppressed since childhood and had sprung back into her heart when Zoran had snuck into her world. She had to win at this. Never before had the stakes been so high. Every night, for the past three days she had been calling Zoran on her cell phone in secret. With their combined efforts, they had slowly pushed both of their families towards the agreement that they should cancel the negotiations and contracts with the other countries. The complexity of these negotiations was mind-boggling, but neither one of them was willing to back down.

Every night, Zoran told her how much he loved her. And she promised that she would not let the situation get out of hand. For three days there was turmoil within all four countries. In the end, the four rulers decided to meet at the Fortress of the Guards, a secret fortress that had stood for centuries and was now nestled in the place where the four corners of their countries met. Their goal was to all come to terms with what had happened over the summer and calm angry tempers.

It was quite shocking to find out that Prince Tasir and Princess Jalayla were in complete agreement with canceling the contracts as well. Both of them had been working on their families separately to try and stop the marriage announcements. When all of the parties were finally together in the enormous conference room at the secret fortress, it was discovered that the marriage negotiations between each of the parties, which had been finalized over the past several months, all needed to be canceled.

With a sigh of relief, all four rulers agreed to cancel the contracts and start new negotiations with the correct couples.

When Zoran heard that everyone was in agreement, he walked out of the conference room and found Ciara in the kitchen sitting with Jalayla. Both women were laughing and sipping white wine while they chuckled over the insanity of how these marriage negotiations had turned out.

As soon as he saw her, he lifted her up into his arms and carried her out of the kitchen, barely taking the time to excuse the two of them from Princess Jalayla. But he wasn't concerned with insulting the beautiful woman. As soon as he carried his own woman out of the kitchen, he saw Prince Tasir walking into the kitchen. The intense look in his eyes told Zoran that the other man was about to do exactly what Zoran was currently doing.

"We're getting married," he said as he carried Ciara down the hallway to his bedroom. Ciara laughed as her arms went around his neck.

"That sounds like a lovely plan, my love."

When the door closed behind him, he looked down into her eyes. "Do you really?"

She knew exactly what he was asking. "Yes. I love you very much. I think you're an extraordinary man and I would be honored to be your wife." She smiled when he bent his head and sealed her promise with a kiss.

"I love you too, my forest nymph. And I won't ever let you go," he promised.

News Flash – October
In an unprecedented month, Crown Prince Zoran del Hassar Alzar of Larcatia has married Princess Ciara bin Sarook of Altair in a fabulous wedding ceremony. And just last week, we saw pictures of the wedding ceremony of Crown Prince Tasir al Sharhi of Lurasa to Princess Jalayla bin Faisal of Tularia. There is a strong hope that the marriages of these four will calm the rising tensions between the various factions that have been arguing for more separation on border operations.

News Flash- April
There are disturbing reports of border fighting among some of the more isolated villages. Unconfirmed deaths are coming into the newsroom. Our reporters are flying out to these areas to discover what's true and what is just rumor. More news about this breaking story to come!

News Flash – June
Continued border fighting has broken out between Larcatia and Tularia as the tension increases. Many villagers are angry at the broken promises and contracts, reacting out of anger. The governments are calling for calm but the villages don't seem to be listening.

News Flash – September (Two years later)
The Tularian government has declared war against Lurasa as violence continues to spread. There are tensions increasing over the oil fields near the borders between Lurasa and Altair and diplomats are scrambling to calm rattled nerves.

News Flash – January
World leaders are converging at The Hague to start peace talks with the governments of Lurasa, Tularia, Altair and Larcatia after fighting broke out in that previously friendly region. Oil prices are rising as the fighting threatens the oil refineries while these four major oil producing countries try to ease the anger and bitterness that has been increasing over the past year although the origins of the violence is still not clear.

Excerpt from The Sheik's Secret Bride, Book 3 in the War, Love, & Harmony Series

"Hello Callie."

Callie heard the deep voice but her arms, still loaded down with the items of daily life, didn't move. Not a muscle in her body moved.

At first her heart soared, excitement ripped through her mind and body. He was here! He came back for her! She almost turned to throw herself into his strong arms, but then the painful memories, the horror and fear of those terrible days in his country....

There was a pause, a pregnant moment when nothing in the world moved. Possibly even the earth stopped rotating because her excitement swiftly changed to paralyzing fear.

That voice. It was impossible! He couldn't be here, she told herself even as her arms started shaking from the effort of holding everything. It simply wasn't possible that he was here. Not this man, not now. Things had been going so well! This man would...well, things would change!

The mail, her purse, computer bag and groceries that had been precariously balanced in her arms suddenly tumbled to the floor as the world mercilessly started moving again. "No!" she whispered with both anguish and that silly, irrational hope that she'd tried very hard to obliterate over the past five years.

As she slowly straightened up, she whispered, "Please, please, please, please," as if her begging could diminish the possibility of that one man with that incredible voice standing in her apartment at this moment.

Life had been going so beautifully lately, she simply would not allow for the possibility that he was standing here. The last time he'd come into her life, her world had become out of control. She'd fallen madly in love with that man and followed him from the United States to his beautiful country. For a few weeks, they'd been deliriously happy and she couldn't believe her luck in finding a man as tall, strong and handsome, wondering what he could possibly see in her. But on a normal trip through the exciting Saturday market where she'd started to learn about

93

his country and the people, she'd been kidnapped, tossed into a dark hole for three days and, at the end of it all, she'd come back to the relative safety of the United States. As if being kidnapped and traumatized, then ripped from the arms of the man she loved more than life itself wasn't bad enough, she'd discovered that she was also alone, homeless and…pregnant.

She'd turned her life around. She now had a job she loved, a warm, comfortable place to come home to every night and friends, not to mention her adorable little boy who gave her so much happiness. Life was good. And no matter how amazing the sex had been with this man, no matter how shockingly wonderful he had made her feel or how alive and vibrant her life had become for those short weeks she'd been in his company, she would never go back to that world. She could never let this man back into her life. She wouldn't do that to her son or to herself.

When she was once again able to breathe, she looked up, almost afraid – maybe afraid that he was here or perhaps that he wasn't. Her mind might be adamant that this man was not coming back into her life, but her body was remembering what it was like to be touched by this man. To be held in his arms. Good grief, just listening to him had been a turn on because of the deep voice that felt like naughty thoughts sliding over her skin whenever he spoke. He could be droning on about oil prices or treaties and her whole body would start tingling. It had been embarrassing the last time they'd been together because he could so easily break down her resistance.

Resistance. That was a laugh, she thought as she slowly turned to find the man through the dim light of the fading afternoon sunlight, praying that it wasn't really him. Because she had zero resistance where this man was concerned. He had powers over her that could make her knees tremble from just a look.

"You're not here," she said to the image standing in her living room. "You can't be here."

Zahir watched the woman that had haunted his dreams as she slowly straightened. She'd lost weight, he noticed. But she was still as beautiful as he remembered. And she still had the most powerful effect on his body just by her presence. He'd never been able to control his body's response to this woman. She was like a drug that had become an addiction to him. A drug he'd had to send away to protect.

But it was safe now. And he was determined to claim his woman.

Her words were soft and her full, pink lips rounded in surprise as she confronted him. Even as he stood there, he couldn't believe how quickly his body hardened just at the sight of her. She was truly beautiful with her thick blond hair and her almost golden eyes. They were actually brown, he remembered, but the golden flecks changed the color, making them appear lighter during certain moods. Her eyes had always fascinated him and he wanted to pull her into his arms right now, make love to her and bring her back to his country so that he could rediscover all those secret places that had fascinated him five years ago.

He restrained from his initial instinct, his need to toss her over his shoulder and carry her out of this place. He had to be careful with her. She'd been traumatized the last time he'd brought her to his home. He would have to show her that she could trust him, prove that she would be safe. As much as he wanted her, in his home and in his bed, proving that she was safe would take time.

"I'm here, Callie," he replied softly, urgently.

She shook her head, a few glossy, golden wisps of hair caressing her neck and shoulders. "No. You're not here."

Zahir moved closer and she stepped back, forgetting the mess surrounding her feet. When she stumbled on her purse, he was quick to reach out and catch her but she pushed his hands away, shaking her head and causing those gorgeous tresses to tumble out of the clip that had been holding them on top of her head. The sunny locks fell down her neck and floated around her shoulders like a golden, silken cloud.

"Don't touch me," she gasped as she found her footing once again. "Just get out of my apartment," she ordered him. She leaned up against the wall, not sure if her legs would hold her upright much longer.

"The war is over," he told her, needing her to know. There was so much he had to tell her, but the most important issue was that the war was over and she would be safe. Safe with him.

Callie stopped cold, her amber eyes sweeping up to his with hope and yearning. "Over?" she whispered. She couldn't believe it. The war had been going on for ten, long, ghastly years! How could it just be over? The trembling that she'd felt initially rushed back with volcanic force, making her fingers shake so badly she had to hide them behind her back, not wanting him to see how intensely that news, as well as his presence, affected her.

He moved a step closer and Callie was stunned anew at how tall he was. And how muscular! And handsome! Goodness, he was so tall and both his height as well as all of those packed muscles on his body never failed to make her feel small and feminine. She'd fought that sensation when they'd first met, thinking she needed to be strong in order to be a woman. But she'd quickly discovered that it was pointless when he was close. Every part of her knew that she was soft and feminine when he was close. Every part of her trembled in anticipation of how he would make all of her femininity scream out with joy and excitement when he was close.

Zahir nodded his dark head, his chestnut brown eyes searching hers and she could see those eyes even in the shadows cast by the descending sun. "Over." He affirmed firmly. "There has been a dramatic change in the leadership of the other three countries over the past few years, which allowed the negotiations to begin. A peace treaty was signed by all four countries last week. It is over."

That news was like a song bursting for joy in her heart, but she mercilessly tamped down that delight. She couldn't believe in the peace, she told herself firmly. She'd naively followed him to his home the last time, thinking that everything would be roses and sunshine. That innocent dream had been shattered when those two disgusting thugs had simply lifted her up as she'd examined the spices in the marketplace, dumping her into the trunk of a car and driving off with her. The guards that had been assigned to protect her hadn't been able to do a thing to stop the abductors, and Callie had been too weak to do anything. Too weak and too scared! But never again! She was stronger now. She was not going to be weak ever again!

Pushing those paralyzing thoughts out of her mind, she confronted him, not even trying to hide the emotions in her body or her tone. "How long?" she asked, her body trembling at the idea of being in his arms again, of being free to love this man. If the war was over then.... "No! It doesn't matter," she said firmly, squinching up her eyes in an effort to get her mind back on the right track. "Wars have stopped and started again. Besides, it is over between us."

Zahir moved closer, his eyes darkening even more as he recognized both her fears and her desires. "The war is over, Callie. And we're going to be together again."

She shook her head, unaware of how that caused her hair to shimmer in the overhead light. "It's never over. You have been at war with your enemies for far too long. Your people don't know how to live with peace. They'll come up with some reason to start fighting again. And I won't go back. I don't want you and I will not endure that life ever again."

He moved closer, hearing her gasp as he put a hand on either side of her head against the wall behind her. He wasn't holding back now. Every fiber of his enormous body emanated the innate authority that had been such a powerful aphrodisiac five years ago. But she fought that feeling, fought against the melting desire to throw herself into his arms and feel his strong muscles hold her gently against his massive chest.

Zahir watched those beguiling amber eyes, seeing everything in them as well as in the subtle movement of her lips and the speeding heartrate on her neck just underneath that soft, tender skin. He would not let her back away from him, though. This was his woman and she had to understand that they were meant to be together. He'd worked hard to get them to this place, and he wasn't going to let her ignore the way she felt for him just because she was scared.

"The war is over. The last of the old guard died six months ago. I've spent every moment since then working with the rulers of the other three countries, building up a peace agreement. That agreement is signed, sealed and delivered. In addition, the people of our countries are sick of wars, sick of their sons and daughters dying. They want peace. They all want to build their towns up again, to live without fear, to walk down the street or go to the market and not be afraid of being attacked. And I'm going to make that happen."

"How?" she demanded. "You saying it won't make it so!" she panicked because he was so close and he smelled so good! Her fingers ached to reach out and touch him, to feel his warm skin and run her fingers across the stubble already forming on his hard jawline. This man, and only this man, could make her feel like this. And she had to fight it. She couldn't go through that again.

Besides, she had Luca to worry about now. She refused to let him be raised in a country where violence was always the answer. He was four years old and the most amazing little man. She was a mother now and she had to protect her child.

She just had to fight against his appeal. She reminded herself that she was stronger now. She'd learned the hard way what could happen when she ignored caution. She could ignore this! She had to! His confidence might make her shiver – as did that voice – but she tamped down those feelings. In the past, those two aspects of this man had been a powerful aphrodisiac, never failing to make her body respond. But right now, she needed to just push him out of her life.

Zahir perceived the battle was waging inside of her and realized that this would be harder than he'd anticipated. His beautiful Callie wasn't the naïve, sweet, trusting woman she'd been five years ago. Oh, she was still shockingly beautiful, so much so that it made him ache to keep his hands off of her. But he had to gain her trust first. That was the most important thing right now.

"The peace will hold. I have secret meetings every three months with the rulers of the other countries involved, more often if something happens to threaten the peace even slightly. It is done. The other three rulers are just as determined to put war behind them as I am. We are all working very hard to rebuild our economies, our cities and villages. We will make this work." he told her forcefully.

She shook her head, both to stop his words as well as to stop the thrilling impact of his nearness. "I don't believe you."

"It is over." His hand moved to her hair, his fingers tangling in her blond tresses. "It's over," he repeated adamantly. "We can get on with our lives."

A moment later, his mouth covered hers. She tried to resist. She truly did. She stood there, trying to not react, to ignore the heart-pounding, desperate need that surfaced with his touch and bubbled throughout her whole body. But this was Zahir. She'd never been able to resist him. Never. And this time was no different.

The kiss went on and on and her whole body pressed against his, needing more than just his lips against her mouth. For five years she'd suppressed her need, ignored her dreams and refused to let herself even think about how he could make her feel. So this kiss, his hands on her waist and her back, made five years of brutally suppressed yearning spring to life inside of her, almost choking her with the need that this man could so effortlessly generate within her.

With a sob, her head tilted forward, resting on his chest. "Don't do this," she begged. "Please, just walk away and pretend that you never saw…me." She almost slipped and told him about Luca but she knew that if he found out about his son, he would never leave here. Five years ago, when she'd been so rapturously happy just being with him, they'd actually talked about children, about how another generation might give his people hope and pull them out of the war.

In response to her pleas, he lifted her head and his mouth covered hers once more. She couldn't stop him and after a moment, she didn't want to. It had been so long, so very long, since a man had touched her. She whimpered, her hands reaching up and clutching the silk of his dress shirt as if it were a life line. She held him there, kissing him and waiting for him to lift her into his arms and carry her to the bedroom, to make love to her as he had so often in the past.

The ringing interrupted them, although she had no idea how long the phone had been going off. He lifted his head, his arm wrapping around her and holding her close, even while she snuggled up against his chest. She was shivering and trying to think creatively about how to handle the situation. She simply couldn't be swept away by this man again. She had to protect their son!

List of Elizabeth Lennox Books

The Texas Tycoon's Temptation

The Royal Cordova Trilogy
Escaping a Royal Wedding
The Man's Outrageous Demands
Mistress to the Prince

The Attracelli Family Series
Never Dare a Tycoon
Falling For the Boss
Risky Negotiations
Proposal to Love
Love's Not Terrifying
Romantic Acquisition

The Billionaire's Terms: Prison or Passion
The Sheik's Love Child
The Sheik's Unfinished Business
The Greek Tycoon's Lover
The Sheik's Sensuous Trap
The Greek's Baby Bargain
The Italian's Bedroom Deal
The Billionaire's Gamble
The Tycoon's Seduction Plan
The Sheik's Rebellious Mistress
The Sheik's Missing Bride
Blackmailed by the Billionaire
The Billionaire's Runaway Bride
The Billionaire's Elusive Lover
The Intimate, Intricate Rescue

The Sisterhood Trilogy
The Sheik's Virgin Lover
The Billionaire's Impulsive Lover
The Russian's Tender Lover
The Billionaire's Gentle Rescue

The Tycoon's Toddler Surprise
The Tycoon's Tender Triumph

The Friends Forever Series
The Sheik's Mysterious Mistress
The Duke's Willful Wife
The Tycoon's Marriage Exchange

The Sheik's Secret Twins
The Russian's Furious Fiancée
The Tycoon's Misunderstood Bride

Love By Accident Series
The Sheik's Pregnant Lover
The Sheik's Furious Bride
The Duke's Runaway Princess

The Russian's Pregnant Mistress

The Lovers Exchange Series
The Earl's Outrageous Lover
The Tycoon's Resistant Lover

The Sheik's Reluctant Lover
The Spanish Tycoon's Temptress

The Berutelli Escape
Resisting The Tycoon's Seduction
The Billionaire's Secretive Enchantress

The Big Apple Brotherhood
The Billionaire's Pregnant Lover
The Sheik's Rediscovered Lover

The Tycoon's Defiant Southern Belle

The Sheik's Dangerous Lover (Novella)

The Thorpe Brothers
His Captive Lover
His Unexpected Lover
His Secretive Lover
His Challenging Lover

The Sheik's Defiant Fiancée (Novella)
The Prince's Resistant Lover (Novella)
The Tycoon's Make-Believe Fiancée (Novella)

The Friendship Series
The Billionaire's Masquerade
The Russian's Dangerous Game
The Sheik's Beautiful Intruder

The Love and Danger Series – Romantic Mysteries
Intimate Desires
Intimate Caresses
Intimate Secrets
Intimate Whispers

The Alfieri Saga
The Italian's Passionate Return (Novella)
Her Gentle Capture
His Reluctant Lover
Her Unexpected Admirer
Her Tender Tyrant
Releasing the Billionaire's Passion (Novella)
His Expectant Lover

The Sheik's Intimate Proposition (Novella)

The Hart Sisters Trilogy
The Billionaire's Secret Marriage
The Italian's Twin Surprise (USA Today™ Best Seller!)
The Forbidden Russian Lover (USA Today™ Best Seller!)

The War, Love, and Harmony Series
Fighting with the Infuriating Prince (Novella)
Dancing with the Dangerous Prince (Novella)
The Sheik's Secret Bride
The Sheik's Angry Bride
The Sheik's Blackmailed Bride
The Sheik's Convenient Bride

The Boarding School Series – September 2015 to January 2016
The Boarding School Series Introduction
The Greek's Forgotten Wife
The Duke's Blackmailed Bride
The Russian's Runaway Bride
The Sheik's Baby Surprise
The Tycoon's Captured Heart

www.ingramcontent.com/pod-product-compliance
Lightning Source LLC
Chambersburg PA
CBHW070222140626
46555CB00018B/1129